Is
Only
Now

An Anthology of 13 Poems
& 5 Short Stories

By Glenn D. Webster

Printed in the United Kingdom
First Printing, 2020

ISBN: 978-1-9163663-0-5 (Paperback)
ISBN: 978-1-9163663-1-2 (eBook)
ISBN: 978-1-9163663-2-9 (Hardback)

Glenn D. Webster
thereisonlynowthebook@hotmail.com

Cover Design Artwork by Glenn D. Webster. Copyright © 2020

Contents

Foreword

We live in a world rich in colour, texture, sound and movement, the detail of which is constantly around us and there for all to see, if only we can look with clear eyes, unclouded and unshackled by mundane thoughts.

In this book of thirteen poems (including one adult poem) and five short stories (including one *Brexit*-themed adult political satire), I have endeavoured to bring to life descriptions, stories and ideas that everyone can relate to, in an anthology which I hope not only entertains but, at its heart, stimulates and enriches the reader's imagination.

Glenn D. Webster
London, November 2019.

This book is dedicated to
Katrina & Ryan.

Gravity

Anchored to this earth knowing what goes up must come down, as Isaac Newton discovered, so we are told, with a wince and a frown, unless you are an astronaut on the International Space Station where everything including water floats around; not unlike the mammoth spinning blue marble in the black, diamond-specked moat, on which skipping children jump, suspended for a split second off the ground.

Living under an invisible ten-foot ceiling but less than that if snuggled up in a tent of an evening, or more than that if on the first floor or higher in a block of flats, walking or running, swinging our limbs forwards and back, moving slower than ants from A to B and on to C, from home to walk, to run, to pogo stick, to bicycle, to motorbike or with knees bent and back straight, to catch a bus, a train or the Tube, or to a space hopper and onto work, including those who do not work and even those who shirk, or out to play or even to go on holiday; to buildings selling our love PET hate plastic swathed consumables, food and drink, or things that advertisers convince us to think we need, heads buried, losing our bottle to non-biodegradable, petroleum-based plastics out of sight, out of mind, in fear of doing what is right, like a scruffy phone and a computer tablet available without prescription, so we can electronically order more cardboard shipping container-encased crap, courier-delivered day or night straight in our lap, electric lightbulbs designed to fail, a bed with hand plucked duck or goose down bedding or of nails and curtains to match, and spectacles to allegedly improve our 20/20 sight, and front door deadbolt mortise locks (more secure than just a latch), and a table and chairs, and crappy inventions like the reversible nappy, or bloody quackers individually-toed duck wellies, and carpeted stairs, and a toxic PVC plastic toothbrush and plastic microbead-filled toothpaste, and a flushing toilet with a sexist and reliable polypropylene moulded seat (and loo rolls with two-ply sheets purchased in haste), blushing at lame excuses for wet wipes and cooking fat selfishly passing through it to congeal and block the sewers, such a shame, and a water boiling machine called a kettle, filled with fresh water from a device called a tap, and flicking a switch for light and turning a dial for heat, and exercising once a week when we run a bath, and even a kitchen sink; and a petrodollar polluting car, poisonous chemical-emitting machines with wheels to move us from A to B to C and to point D, because to bounce there is too far, and computer machines to send urgent email messages to point E instantly, instead of gathering our thoughts to compose a heartfelt letter, delivered by post and then personally by hand – far better, and fridge freezer machines to chill and freeze our food, and oven machines to cook it, if not tempted to order a takeaway and when we're in the mood, and vacuum machines to clean up our dead skin detritus mess, and flat screen television machines displaying visual images in 2D or not 2D (*that* is the question) with inescapable surround sound, or old black and white TV sets that are apparently still hanging around, so we can watch others do the same or, preferably undisturbed with recyclable aluminium can of beer in hand, the game!

Unlike the enviable honey bee that flies unaided from flowers back to the hive so naturally, as we board larger machines to transport us to foreign shores and then return home, grounded by our undetectable and undetachable ball and chain as invisible gravity glues us, once again, to footfall on the floor, while others attached who we never meet walk just like us in lands afar, putting their feet alternately one in front of the other: place weight, release back, step forward, place weight and repeat, only they do it barefoot on rocks, on soil, on mud and on sand, or squatting, practise open defecation, with no doors left ajar.

In contrast, our land is concrete and bricks enveloping everything we need to drink or eat or clothe our bodies in, like a glass of tap water, a cup of tea, a bottle of wine or a malt whisky from a single distillery instead, and waking up to the intoxicating smell of freshly baked bread and hot buttered toast with a full English or troked for eggy soldiers dunked in a runny yolk and bubble and squeak, sausage and mash, roasted seasonal vegetables from a local farmers' market, or better still, a local farmer; a post-mortem battered fish with mushy peas and chips or fingers from a genetically modified fish, in a butty, or brightly lit, freezer shelf-stacked, cellophane-wrapped beef rump steak, or llama, seared in lard and lathered in English mustard, in repose while frying eggs, salt and peppered, lay on top, or a succulent leg of lamb butchered from slaughter, braised in its natural juices with gravy and served with mint jelly, tablespoon-scooped out of the jar with a *sshlup*, just sublime! – and furry slippers and lace-up shoes, and embroidered studded leather horse hair thongs, and crotchless corrugated thermal long johns, and nipple tassels to amuse, and tuxedos and dickie bows and top hat and tails and fancy dresses, and passing the port from your right to the left, like in the navy, or drinking tea with a raised pinkie, and travelling by carbon-emitting private jet, offsetting the debt with carbon credit smoke and mirrors, I bet, transporting carbon footprint-reducing ballerinas with en pointe feet to entertain the jet set elite; in fact, all of our la-di-da excesses, not including a Courvoisier brandy with a Montecristo No. 2 Cuban cigar and a classic Jaguar, purchased with printed paper and coin called cash, or four digits uniquely in a row, electronically confirming hassle-free payment from banks via plastic cards, so easy to lose!

Theirs is fire struck from stone or hand-drilled by friction, gutted kill deboned and thrown on flat, heated rock, crouching and adding kindling with stick in hand, prodding white wood embers to stop the flame from dwindling, and blowing breath to fan and grow the flame, to heat and cook the bush meat, served atop a large evergreen leaf with huge, fat, white bugs, nutritious, prised out from underneath a fallen tree, deep in the bark, collected in a torrential basin with dribbling smiles and, once tasted, rated *'Delicious!'* by men and women and children who have never seen or touched a plastic carrier bag, but recount in whispered rhymes the story of that one time when, swimming offshore with spear submerged while hunting fish, in the current one drifted past, spear tip twisted at last to catch, and after striding out across jagged rocks beneath, their dad sat crouching as he unwrapped it from around the obsidian spear tip at his feet, an orange plastic bag, brought in luggage, airplane-flown, by a holiday maker from a distant home, who used it to carry bread and milk, and cabbage, cauliflower and potatoes, and meat, cheese and eggs, and oranges, apples and pears and bananas, and coriander and thyme and a winning lottery ticket, *fantastic!*

Now reused to carry fish and crabs as, spear in hand, the dripping dad looks from a distance like a weird Sainsbury's supermarket advert promoting their new gratis 'Catch & Keep' underwater store, *SUBSISTENCE*, where if fish are caught and crabs and lobster too through sheer persistence, there is no charge, as you place your snapper into a matching plastic carrier bag, not a lattice basket, with little resistance.

Out of depth, treading water, legs egg whisk forward and back, trained eyes looking down into the ocean depths through a mask, for this is a rare moment with which most will never be tasked, as distance measured above the head or below the feet are vast, until once again land meets wet soles of feet placed at last, and man, woman and child are ground magnetised back to walk under the invisible ten-foot ceiling, passing by people fishing from the shore, a straining man excitedly bent at his bowing rod reels in an orange snapper, only to see more plastic bags wrapped around his tackle than ever before!

Disconnected Out

Who am I?

Nobody special because I'm not online; only living peacefully, anonymously sublime.

Search me up, fill your cup! Look, not a trace, so place your stake, I must be a fake!

People jockeying, fighting for position, kissing both cheeks, best friends of just two weeks, recommended by supercilious sycophants who reek of desperation, yearning for a leg-up; more money means more power, foot in stirrup and back turned, they ride off without a word or a wave, never to see you again, this well-tailored knave, of no concern!

Five hundred connections, yet ironically more disconnected than ever before! I consider half a dozen people to be friends, but it's probably half of that if truth be told; so, brag about the hundreds you 'know,' and catapult yourself while selling your soul, for in the sands of time when your ship is holed, those 'friends' will disappear like burrowing moles!

Disconnect to reconnect with your life, your children, your partner, your husband, your wife; live in the now, communicating face to face at your own pace, and see what was intended, not trapped under capitalism's yoke pretended!

Leave the flock, turn back the clock, immerse in the real and cut your own deal stealing back your life; hijacked and hornswoggled by the banks in the middle of the night, convincing innocents of the beauty of a debt ridden existence!

Hold my hand, look into my eyes and say everything in the silence of a promised land, with crystal rivers and ancient trees, and bottomless seas lapping at golden sands; vast expanse of beach, a plain of sand and blue-ceilinged sea, open and empty, walk with me.

Place your coat around your partner's shoulders and rejoice in their warmth, your hunger; shivering at the thought of a life devoid of love and care for another, alone, isolated to the bone, as huge-winged albatross snuggle up to a destiny mate, a partner to die for, a solitary gliding speck at sea for months their lot, sacrificing their need to be together, a nestling family on a clifftop windswept aloft, a must, not shot and swung around a sailor's neck; unaware, we humans may scoff at their indefatigability without the promise of a crust.

The Horse and
the Tree

'Hello tree,' said the horse.

The tree did not reply.

'What is it like being a tree?' asked the horse, its ears tilted forward.

The tree was silent, as it thought about how it might answer such a difficult question.

'I love being a horse,' said the horse.

The tree wondered why that was and contemplating the statement remained silent.

'Don't you get bored, just stood in the same place all day every day?' asked the horse.

The tree thought about that but was still contemplating what it must be like being a horse.

'One of the reasons why I love being a horse is because I can run and jump around,' said the horse enthusiastically.

The tree had no idea what the horse was talking about because it had never moved, let alone ran or jumped, but it decided to remain silent rather than contradict the horse with the opposite opinion.

'How old are you?' asked the horse.

The tree was old, very old. In fact, the tree was much older than the horse, but rather than explain that it was old enough not to care, the tree just stood looking at the horse.

If you had legs, we could run and jump together,' said the horse.

The tree liked the idea, but knew that it did not need to run anywhere, and it certainly did not need to jump and thinking about the horse's four legs, it didn't want to upset the horse by explaining that it not only had many more legs than the horse, all of which were running underground, it also had many outstretched arms that it could wave around.

The horse stepped forward as its tail lifted in the breeze and, raising itself up on its hind legs, it stretched out its front legs, resting its hooves on the tree's sun-blotched mossy trunk and looked up into the rustling bough canopy, with its tangled mesh crown of variegated foliage. It saw that the tree was really tall and, dropping its legs down, it moved in closer and rubbed its mane against the tree's fissured bark, back and forth, while snorting with pleasure.

The tree did not move, but it felt the horse's hooves and it felt the horse's hide, and it was pleased that the horse could scratch itself.

'Well, I really enjoyed talking to you,' said the horse, and turning, it walked back across the field from where it had come.

So did I, thought the tree, waving goodbye but remaining silent.

People, Poor
People Poor

People populate this planet, but so do penguins, pandas, parakeets, porcupines, pelicans, pythons, porpoises, parrots, polar bears, possums, panthers, partridges, praying mantis, piranhas, puffins, peacocks, potbellied pigs and parasites.

People eat animals and animals sometimes eat people, but all animals eat one another!

People also keep animals as pets, and while most people pet their pets and others personify them, some people imprison their pets and even eat them, which is not just predatory, but peculiarly pernicious!

There are also pets that eat other people's pets, which is pitiful!

They say some people also eat people, but I think that is probably a perverse, pessimistic parable.

How pathetic we are though, masticating in our pyjamas as we pig out! Pedantic, peremptory people pontificating about a pepperoni pizza; filling our persons with pulverised processed pork and beef, purveyor-pounded and sliced into puny circles of piquant perfection.

Polish off your petulant pride and prejudicial pulpit pandering, pallescent, full-bellied philistine, and preserve your fit of pique for those poor people who precariously pick particles from parchment, as dusk dwindles and a weeping pregnant mother commits peaceful pauper perjury, squatting by a paltry flame, her padella parboiling pabulum pebbles to persuade her poorly-provisioned, pandiculating, potbellied children of the lie that food is nigh!

Pontificate about these peoples' poor plight, and proudly persuade others that their patronage be sowed and pragmatically ploughed proper, for some have no purpose but to pander to their personal, pusillanimous prism of pleasure and parsimonious, precious profit; pathetic perpetrators producing a preserved, patented paradigm of putrid pork belly pancetta!

Percolate your mind with truth and your heart with love, the panacea of all time, for we are all penurious peasants, anchored to the land and sea from whence we came and thereby pay, not alike but identical in every way.

Seaside Seagulls

Seaside seagulls in flight overhead, bright sunlit white, big as dogs, wings unfurled with custard-coloured beaks, legs and feet, hovering kites in the blue, desperate to be fed.

Heads turning searching for a bite, swooping down one gives me a fright as I crouch, it nicks my beef sandwich and my finger.

'*Ouch!*' Pain lingers, but I don't need a bandage,

'Oi, bastard!' pardon my language!

'Caw-caw!' response.

'I hope you choke on the mustard!'

Hop, run, scoff, fly aloft.

I'd chase after you if I was younger, but I just stand with my sore bloody finger and silently ponder, *Is possession not nine tenths of the law?*

Good question, thieving monger, is that your brief or just your last straw to hunger?

Gulp, it's gone, starts searching, 'Caw-caw!' translated from Seagull it means, 'More! More!'

Now rejoined its greedy gang of gliding pirates, rising up on hot air above the pregnant deckchair-freckled shore, as I look on while sucking the wound at exactly half-past noon, watching brightly dressed day trippers crowd the beach, a rainbow food fest from up high: hot dogs, burgers, fish and chips, don't be shy, as an ice cream vendor leans over his serving hatch to plop a chocolate flake into a grinning child's 99'er, almost out of reach.

Neck Bent,
Senses Spent

I see them shuffling along, an army of screen-hypno-
tised robots, neck bent, head down with a frown, ear
plugs blocking out what's around, world sound; stepping blindly into a road, cyclists reach for the brake,
car tyres screech, horns honking, as they bump into
lamp posts on auto pilot mode!

Ignoring the Ash, Horse Chestnut, Silver Birch or
Oak, oblivious to Cumulus, Nimbostratus, Cirrus
Uncinus or Fractus.

What?

Is that a joke?

Ironically blinded to everything in front of their eyes, except the superglued screen in their hands, a portal, an I spy.

Remind me of what is in front, above, below, behind?

Why?

I'm not in the mood!

Perceived knowledge of a world apart, a far cry.

Someone somewhere lit a fart! Capture, engage, react, pass it on, start a craze, not in the beauty of the world in front of your face, or the taste of a freshly caught grilled plaice, no, rejoice in detached personal owner-ship of something, someone, somewhere, contrived in a distant place, like a camouflaged soy-coloured frog sat deep in an Amazonian jungle bog, jumping for joy at Parisian chefs awarded best frogs legs, proudly paraded above their heads, related if not connected, chasing entertainment value instead!

Don't commit or employ your time, energy, attention, hard work, spit, blood, grit, sweat, care, tears, love and money, just sit back and stare at something, anything, honey! It might be sweetly unfair bad luck, but personally funny; who cares, it doesn't affect me or my life because, like a car crash, we steer passed and stare, not me or us but them, and so after a glib, 'Oh dear, how unfair!' we continue on unaffected and in the clear, pressing send to our five thousand friends who need to hear!

Shame on us for allowing our children, our siblings, to be conned by a hand-bonded screen, feeding their lust for knowledge by irrelevant and irreverent means, laden with unseen lies and hate, but wait! I didn't know those people were being indiscriminately killed! Stop, filter, engage brain, the innocent are all the same: innocent, not pop stars vying for recognition, money and fame!

Look at me making a cup of tea!

Why?

Good news travels, but bad news travels fast and far, like a butterfly released from a jar, the beauty of it crushed underfoot, making us shut up as we stare at the screen and tut-tut press a button and pass on another blip, shooting from the hip, devouring a burger and ingesting the merger of self-gratification and zero accountability, watching from a distance with shameful civility as people of a poor nation scramble for sustenance, our poor relations, while ketchup-covered onion falls onto our chest and we moan that we've ruined our shirt, our blouse, our vest, our best silk tie, which others would twist to support a broken wrist, or pinch as an integral part of a pulley and winch!

So, prepare yourself and plan ahead to gain and prosper by training to be a chiropractor, for future neck pains of once-young people now aged will doubtless be great business thereafter!

Picky Park Pond

Sailing my boat on *Picky* Park pond, as tadpoles
wiggle and wallow in slime green shallows, and trans-
lucent, jellied, black-eyed frog spawn just stares back,
poor fellows,

while sticklebacks hover with aggressive intent,

the wind sending ripples to toss my yacht, over which
I'm bent,

raindrops splatter *plop-plop-plop*, heaven sent,

hopping to take flight are glossy black crows,

raven storm clouds barrelling as strong wind blows, it
will not relent,

me huddling next to my dad in his sheepskin coat, as
big as a tent,

boat sail flapping, dry docked in my hands,

rain starts lashing at my face as we stand,

water droplets running down my nose,

golf umbrella unfurled overhead, as I wonder what it must be like to sleep underwater without a bed; owner chases barking dog chasing crows,

light dimmed dismal, dodging puddles back to our Austin 1100,

slamming the doors to the first lightning and cracking thunder!

Key turned, heater blasting, squeaking wipers waving, slapping water,

everlasting thermos coffee piping hot, rising water vapour, blowing breath ripples shorter,

misted windows, hand-wiped wet,

warming up, but not dry yet,

looking out, chucking it down, raining cats and dogs,
soaked concrete dark,

silky iron park gates black as coal, deserted pond
chopping alone, skating puddle bubbles popping,

countless raindrops rat-a-tat-tat-tapping car roof above,
bouncing like spears on stone, on water dancing.

Drenched park warden approaching, stern-faced meet
and greet,

trudging across glass-glossy grass with muddy feet
sploshing,

dad looks angry, passes me his drink,

out of the car, challenges dripping peak-capped
jobsworth, I'm tickled pink!

Muffled words from moving mouths lost, as shocked
warden backs off,

his verbal warning,

'Not allowed to park there!'

no joke, the only cost,

feeling my heart beating,

dad soaked but victorious, back in driver's seat,

big hands cup his coffee, telling me not to worry, as
we watch dour dictator slip-sliding up soggy grass
bank from afar, only to fall facedown,

dad spit spraying coffee all over the car,

identical in colour to mud-covered parky star,

me laughing so much it hurts, as dad ready to blurt
opens his door, steps out, left ajar,

'Oi, you're not allowed to fall there!' he shouts, as bespattered warden picks up his cap, now mad, and turning about, V signs my dad, who climbs back in guffawing, sits saturated, slamming the door with me teary-eyed; coffee-stained lap coughing, as we drive off for home towards the park gates a *KEEP OFF THE GRASS* sign we see sends us scoffing!

What an adventure, I can't wait to tell my mates!

There Is Only Now

There is only now to capture somehow this moment, suspended but ended,

to live in the beat of your heart, as the second hand sweeps what may be intended,

so push on with that thought, and gallop henceforth to chase what ought to be splendid,

for no one who lived has ever misgiven the truth of regretting missed chances from heaven,

fallen in your lap unforeseen, but fugacious forthwith, a has-been.

Now snatch and grab your transient time tab without hesitation,

to dither is to wilt is to wither,

so plunge your needs to the hilt, as ambivalence is slain to silt,

destroy your perceived guilt which others have built, and halting clock's lot,

wallow yourself like a mud-revelling hippo, whose time is nigh and cares not a jot!

Order! Order!
(Adult)

House of ~~Commons~~ Comedians, MP's Canteen Dining Hall, Houses of Parliament, London.

Friday, 24th May 2019.

'OR-DER! OR-DER!'

'Please order.'

'Oh yes, sorry. May I have the haddock, thank you.'

'At last, a prime minister who can actually make a decision,' the dinner lady replies, smiling sarcastically as she serves Theresa May her lunch in the House of Commons canteen dining hall.

'When it comes to my stomach, I am as decisive as a praying mantis,' May says, turning to Member of Parliament Ian Blackford, Leader of the Scottish National Party, who is stood next to her in the lunch queue, smiling politely.

'Except our food is already dead and cooked,' dinner lady remarks.

'Rather than alive and raw, you mean?' May asks.

'Exactly!'

'Well, I do have a reputation for eating people alive, don't I, Mr Blackford?'

'Oh yes, quite the reputation, Prime Minister,' he replies, blushing as the dinner lady smiles awkwardly.

'If last night's European election results are anything to go by, it looks like Farage has eaten you alive!' dinner lady quips.

'Oh, very good, yes, ha-ha!' Blackford chortles.

'There is nothing like a lovely fillet of haddock,' May says, looking down at the battered fish on her plate with obvious disappointment, 'and this is *nothing like* a lovely fillet of haddock.' She scowls at the dinner lady with heavy-lidded eyes as she sidles along the counter. 'Oh, and by the way, just so you know,' she stops abruptly and eyeballs the dinner lady.

'What is it now?' dinner lady asks, pouting sullenly, hand tightly gripping the stainless steel, perforated metal chip scoop, as she stares back at May.

'You've got a bloody chip on your shoulder,' May says, jabbing a pointed finger!

'You what? Look who's talking!' the mardy, crumpled-faced dinner lady replies.

'No, honestly, you've got a chip on your shoulder,' May repeats, pointing at the pinkie-sized chip resting on the dinner lady's left shoulder.

'What? Oh, really?' dinner lady questions, glancing at her shoulder-supported fried chipped potato. 'Oh yes – well, I never! How the hell did that get there, I wonder. Thank you, Prime Minister!' embarrassed dinner lady says, brushing the chip off onto the floor.

'When the chips are down,' May says with a wink.

'For a second there, Prime Minister, I thought you were *codding*!' dinner lady retorts, grinning.

'"Codding?" What do you- ah yes, I get it. Good one!' May allows, shuffling along towards the till smiling, as Ian Blackford MP takes her plaice.

'I'm rather peckish myself, and somewhat parched, I have to say, so I'll also have the chish and fips as well please, but could I have the hod instead of the caddock,' Blackford asks, smiling, in a poor attempt at ingratiating humour.

'You've obviously forgotten to wear your court jester outfit,' dinner lady smirks.

'Oh yes, ha-ha!' Blackford chuckles. 'All joking aside, though, it's two for the price of one, isn't it?' he asks hopefully.

'No!' dinner lady answers emphatically.

'Oh dear, never mind! Well, here's my fish Friday loyalty card, fully stamped, so I believe I'm entitled to a free double portion of mushy peas? Could I also have a deep-fried Mars bar please, a slice of lemon, a portion of tartare sauce and some HP?' He hands over his card, grinning, as he returns his wallet to the inside pocket of his suit jacket. 'Oh, and I'll also have a bottle of Irn-Bru and, erm, do you have a new card and a stamp as well please?'

'It's *one* free portion of *Trumpton* pushy meas! We only serve deep-fried chish, not chocolate bars! We've run out of lemons, except those stood with you in the queue, and you can say ta-ra to the tartare. It's cash on delivery, not HP. There's no Irn-Bru, bro, and you can get a new loyalty card stamped on by stiletto till girl after you pay, and don't forget the partridge in a pear tree, Mr Fussy Britches!'

'Ah, oh well, thank you anyway!' Blackford blushes and retreats despondently, taking his plated chish and fips with *one* portion of pushy meas lunch from the dinner lady, and placing it on his tray.

'Can we please hurry up, Mr Tight Arse,' Speaker of the House John Bercow butts in, stood next to and nudging Blackford from the side, 'I'm about to eat my own foot!'

'You're the one having the duck, Mr Speaker,' Blackford responds wryly.

'Ah yes, watertight. Very droll.'

'You do have a habit of putting *your* foot in your mouth,' Theresa May interrupts, glancing at Bercow with raised eyebrows, as she finishes paying for her lunch and waits for her loyalty card to be stamped.

'I think you're confusing me with the leader of the opposition,' Bercow replies.

'Touché!' May concedes.

'Next please!' dinner lady shouts over the chatter.

'I heard that, Bercow, you big gob!' comes a voice from behind.

'Ah, Mr Corbyn, ears as keen as our coastal defence system, eh?' Bercow turns to Leader of the Labour Party Jeremy Corbyn MP, who is stood waiting, tray in hand, further down the queue. 'Your foghorn of a voice can be heard in bloody Calais,' Corbyn says irritably.

'I'll take that as a compliment.'

'Insult, you mean?'

'Skin as thick as a male Rhino's, sorry.'

'His arse, your face!'

'Somewhat below the belt, Jeremy.'

'I was aiming for your Crown Jewels.'

'Balls of steel, I'm afraid!'

'Is it a bird? Is it a plane? No! It's Super Berk!'

'Ladies, please, we are all waiting to be served, so can we stop bickering and hurry up and move along!' ex-Prime Minister David Cameron interjects.

'Oh, if it isn't Cameron the Calamitous,' May blurts out, looking back down the queue and eyeballing Cameron with pure disdain.

'What did you say, May?'

'You heard, Brexit bollocks.'

'Yes, and who took the bloody reins?'

'As we gallop over the fuckin' cliff!'

'Language, Prime Minister!'

'Oh, piss off back to your garden hut, Mr Gnome!'

'Can we please order and move on, for goodness' sake?' Nigel Farage MEP barks from further back down the line. 'I've got a bloody Eurostar to catch!'

'And what the fuck are you doing here, pigeon head?' May shouts, head snapping forward as she looks daggers at Farage. 'Piss off back to Brussels and stay there!'

'I will do once you piss off as PM.'

'Not until this lot support my deal, don't you know.'

'What deal? It's a bleedin' treaty, you daft cow!'

'The deal of the century!'

'You mean *Steal* of the century?'

'I'm not Nicholas bloody Parsons!'

'No, you're his twin.'

'What do you want, Farage? A bloody speed boat and a matching set of stainless-steel steak knives?'

'No, I just want to leave the EU, like the rest of the electorate who won the bloody democratic vote.'

'Mere puff, dear boy, mere puff!'

'Bloody hell, this is turning into *The Great Remain Robbery!*'

'ORDER! OR-DER!' Bercow cries. 'Would the procrastinating prime minister and the pusillanimous pudding head please come to order!'

'Give it a rest, Bercow, you bellowing bollock,' May snaps. 'You're in the lunch queue now, not sat in your bloody House of Commons high chair.'

'GOOGOO GAGGA!' Farage quips.

'Shut it, fuck face,' Bercow blasts Farage.

'I think you actually mean, "Sale of the Century,"
Prime Minister,' Corbyn offers meekly, as May tut-tuts,
rolling her eyes and mouthing the word 'Twat!'

'Well said, granddad,' Farage compliments Corbyn,
as Cameron steps up closer, hands in trouser pockets,
lunch tray tucked under his arm and leaning forward
starts to sing.

'Granddad, we hate you, Granddad we do!' swaying
from side to side, smirking.

'That's bloody slander, Little Lord Fauntleroy,' Corbyn
hits back, voice wavering.

'Hey JC, right or left?' Cameron asks.

'Right what?'

'Right it is!'

BIFF! Cameron socks Corbyn in the kisser, dropping
him like a sack of King Edwards as his tray clatters
to the floor.

'Yeah, the Brexit Bastard strikes again!' he exclaims, standing astride a floored Corbyn, hands on hips and head thrown back in uncontrollable laughter, like a fat, wobbly-cheeked cherub at the point of ejaculation.

'Are you on crack?' Bercow screams, dropping his lunch tray as he launches himself across six feet of highly polished veneer flooring and slams Cameron in the chest, sending him flying backwards into an array of diners, as plates, cutlery, food and drink are catapulted in every direction, and the table beneath Cameron's concussed, dark blue-suited frame collapses to the floor.

'You little fucker!' May screeches, already running towards a fallen chair, and with a skip, hop and a jump she launches herself through the air, elongated horizontally with straight legs, impacting the back of Bercow's head, slamming him into an English oak wood panel, wall-mounted oil painting of Winston Churchill with an almighty CRACK! as the speaker slides down to kiss the deck, leaving his two front teeth embedded in Mr Churchill's mouth, transforming him into a bald-headed Bugs Bunny lookalike!

May starts robot dancing in front of the bewildered diners, laughing hysterically, unaware that Farage has already grabbed a tray and he is prepared to use it.

'Leave it, Nigel, she's not worth it!' former MP George Galloway advises, trying to grab the back of Farage's suit jacket, but it's too late, as Farage is already in frisbee throwing mode and, legs splayed for balance, he hurtles the lacquered Formica spinning towards a guffawing May, who, more by good luck than good judgement, but with perfect timing nevertheless, bends over to offer a robotic hand to comatose Cameron, as the tray flies over and past her to lodge in the back of Vince Cable's minestrone soup-slurping head.

BAM! Soup spoon drops, clattering to the floor, and broth dribbles out of frozen, open-mouthed and eyes-glazed Liberal Democrats leader Cable, as his arms and head flop downwards, shoulders sagging, and his mush meets the minestrone with a loud *SPLOSH*! The tray protruding upwards from his cracked skull, standing vertically proud like some sort of blank restaurant specials board.

'Yeah, good bloody riddance!' ex-Lib Dems leader Nick 'I used to be indecisive, but now I'm not so sure' Clegg yells from an adjacent table, sat half on, half off his chair, dressed casually in an *I'M A TWAT*! Facebook-logoed t-shirt and flip-flops, the irony of his choice of footwear not going unnoticed by visiting American politician, John 'Jimmy Hill chin' Kerry, and also ex-eagle-eyed newspaper editor Nick Ferrari, who is covering the visit for national radio.

All hell breaks loose as Deputy Leader of the Labour Party Tom Watson MP, crouching to the aid of Corbyn, turns his attention to robot dancing May – still 'Brexit Bollocks' rapping over an unconscious Cameron – and with incredible agility, kneecaps her with a crunching side kick.

'Brummie bastard!' she yelps, crumpling to the floor, while Farage starts leather brogue laying into Brylcreemed Cameron's roasted cauliflower and cheese-covered suited torso, as Corbyn, supported by Brummie Basher Watson, rises cross-eyed with a beautifully throbbing, perfect-looking black eye, only to then slump back down next to bloodied Bercow.

'Hey, what the fuck is your problem, tortoise neck?' a stentorian voice shouts at Farage from across the dining hall.

Farage looks up, dripping in sweat from his Conservative kick fest, to see a shirt-sleeved Tony Blair staring back at him. 'What are you doing here, jug ears?' he asks derisively.

'Can't keep away, old boy. Fingers in pies, poke you in the eyes,' former Prime Minister Blair answers loudly with a sickening smile, as he strides over, fists clenched and hips twisting to squeeze between tables towards Farage, who is now stood opposite the canteen serving hatch, *boing-boing* bouncing with adrenaline, unaware that Nick Clegg has left his sedentary position and is flip-flopping to the aid of his battered bum chum Cameron, with his buddy Nick 'Mr Bumble' Ferrari in tow, microphone in hand, being chased by gabbling eager beaver Diane Abbott MP.

'So, that's an extra one thousand pounds over ten years for two hundred and fifty thousand extra police, Mr Ferrari,' Abbott explains. 'That's seven hundred and fifty million a month, multiplied by, sorry, erm, oh yes, so that's five hundred pounds a month divided by one billion, minus-'

Both Clegg and Ferrari are unknowingly and unwittingly blocking Blair's path, until a swift knee dead leg from TB sends NC to the floor!

'And stay down, you Spanish speaking, paella eating prick!' Blair snarls.

'Ooh, you just got ROASTED!' Abbott squeals, wagging her index finger diva-style at floored Clegg, as a gritted-teethed Blair circumnavigates the shocked Ferrari.

'Mr Blair, that- that is physical assault,' Ferrari stammers. 'What- what the bloody hell do you think you're doing? Any comment?'

'Yes, Labour would increase police numbers by, erm, by-'

'Please, Ms Abbott, I'm talking to Mr Blair,' Ferrari cuts her off, exasperated. 'Give it a bloody rest will you! Now, Mr Blair, any comment?'

'No, sorry, I must move on, and only for time reasons,' Blair says, before brain bashing Mr Bumble in the belfry, also decking him, prompting Diane Abbott MP to kneel down next to the recumbent radio presenter and, calculator in hand, she snatches Ferrari's microphone and continues rabbiting on about police numbers and budgets, furiously pressing calculator keys as she digs herself into the biggest hole in the known universe!

Blair pauses for a moment to reload his shirt-sleeved biceps in true Henry Cavill style, before continuing towards Farage, who is now jigging from one foot to the other, up and down in anticipation, while gesticulating *'Come and have a go if you think you're hard enough,'* until a firm hand on the erstwhile PM's right shoulder instantly stops his progress, spinning him around and asking, 'Remember me?'

Blair turns snow white, as media mogul Rupert Murdoch grabs him by the shoulders with both hands and simultaneously knees him in the clems.

BOOF!

Farage cheers as Blair collapses pigeon-toed with an, 'OOOOWWWHH!' while holding his Wendi wand and the twins in both hands.

'Back-stabbing pommy prick!' Murdoch spits venom-ously, as Blair goes down cross-eyed, and he quickly snatches his plate of king prawn chow mein from the table behind and, crouching down next to Blair, slams his Asian cuisine lunch into his contorted face, twisting it left and right! 'You like Chinese, don't you, Tony? So, have it!' Murdoch screams, cackling!

Farage is pissing himself, as Galloway stands next to him with one arm around his shoulder and the other punching the air.

'Yeah, fucker, now that's what you call a Chinese takeaway!' Galloway cheers and smiles at Farage, who is laughing so hard that it looks like his head will explode.

'Wait one bloody minute, you bunch of shandy-drinking sassenachs!' former Prime Minister Gordon Brown bellows, charging at Murdoch and blindsiding him with a rugby tackle into a group of helpless diners!

'Holy shit, this is getting seriously out of hand!' the Archbishop of Canterbury Justin Welby remarks to John Kerry, who is now sat devouring a cheeseburger and fries next to cool as a cucumber, napkin tucked into shirt collar, minestrone soup-sipping Jacob Rees-Mogg MP. Michael, drinking piping hot tea from a teacup and saucer, *Joe 90'* misted glasses, Gove MP and 'Father of the House' Ken Clarke MP, the latter sat with crossed legs stretched out on the chair opposite, digesting a large lunch and raising his eyebrows in a *'Who gives a monkey's uncle?'* expression, while nursing a wonderful sherried, light butterscotch, smoky Glenfarclas fifteen-year-old Scottish single malt whisky. The drink balanced precariously atop his rotund stomach, as he draws on his deliciously rich-flavoured *Hoyo de Monterrey* Double Corona Cuban cigar, exhaling the thick smoke without a care in the world.

'This is the best entertainment I've had since the New York Mets beat the Baltimore Orioles in the sixty-nine World Series!' Kerry declares between mouthfuls. 'As your good old Brucie would say, "Good game! Good game!"' he says, chin jutting out, impersonating Bruce Forsyth, as he wipes his smiling, ketchup-covered mouth with a napkin, eliciting hearty laughter from Rees-Mogg, Gove and Clarke, who all start guffawing!

The Archbishop, now standing, starts rolling up the sleeves of his cassock and robe, secures his Harry Potter glasses behind his ears and picks up and puts on his yellow, turquoise fish-embossed mitre, adjusting it with both hands to snugly grip his head, and then grabbing his golden, solid English oak shepherd's crook leaning against his chair, he leaps up onto the tabletop to survey the battlefield. 'I need to gather my flock and bring them home,' he says out loud to no one in particular, as Ken Clarke looks up at him astride the table with raised eyebrows, exhaling more cigar smoke.

'Constitutionally speaking, you are on very thin ice, Mr Welby,' Rees-Mogg warns. 'Gossamer butterfly wing-thin, in fact!'

Burger-munching Kerry, tea-drinking *'Joe 90'* Gove and cigar-chomping Clarke all nod in agreement, with the latter leaning forward to tap the ash from the end of his Cuban into a nearby ashtray.

'Of course, if you are genuinely unhappy about the situation and you would like to complain, may I suggest writing to your local MP?' Gove advises the Archbishop, glancing upwards and pausing with puckered lips, before taking another sip of tea.

The others nod in agreement once again, as Kerry dabs his mouth with his napkin. 'Oh, and before you go,' the American adds, *'Let's have a look at the old scoreboard!'* he says, chin jutting out in full Brucie impersonation mode again, as the table roars with laughter.

'Go get 'em, caped crusader!' Clarke jeers, leaning back as Noggin the Nog launches himself in the direction of Farage and Galloway, like some sort of futuristic, yellow-helmeted, golden crook-wielding superhero.

Striding table to floor, floor to table, the Archbishop's attention is now focussed on fighting off a large gang of Labour and Conservative backbenchers encroaching on his path, who have upturned tables and unscrewed table legs, and are marching towards isolated Farage and Galloway, makeshift weapons held aloft, chanting, 'Brexit bastards! Brexit bastards!' which Welby accomplishes with a swinging, bludgeoning, accuracy, as he chastises his flock, baton twirling his shepherd's crook across the dining hall!

Luckily, Farage has a plan, and crouching down low, he picks up Galloway from around his ankles and by the belt on his trousers, and launches the diminutive Scot up and over the food counter backwards, like he's tossing the caber, sending Galloway disappearing from view with an '*ARRRRGH!*' accompanied by the sound of smashing crockery and clattering, spinning metal lids. Not far behind, Farage then dives over to join his fallen comrade, landing headfirst next to a crouching, hide-and-seek playing, cream cake-devouring Ian Blackford, whose cream-covered face resembles a teenager's poor first attempt at a wet shave.

'Blughdy loughley cramme caghkeas!' Blackford reports, overflowing gorged gob full of cream cakes.

'Save your breath, Fatty Arbuckle. I don't understand a word you say in the Commons, so I've got no bloody chance now!' Farage snaps, turning to assist Galloway, as stuffed-hamster-cheeked Blackford dolphin smiles back.

Suddenly, the light from the dining hall entrance dims, as a shadow-casting, St George's cross t-shirt-wearing, faded white patched blue jeans and white trainers-clad figure appears in the doorway, armed with a neck-wrapped nunchaku held at chest height.

'Shit a brick!' Gordon Brown gasps, squinting rapidly, 'It's Tommy fucking Robinson!'

Dancing queen Theresa May has now stopped her robot routine and appears frozen to the spot until her head starts to turn slowly towards Farage and Galloway, like a red-lipped rusting Cyberman, both now peeking over the top of the food counter, as she slams Watson's Brummie bonce into the veneered floor for a sixth and final time, before relinquishing her grip and raising the knee that was crushing his lower back and rising up, she nonchalantly spits out the chunk of Corbyn's left ear that she was chewing on with a *PTOO!*, sending the bloody flesh arcing into the countertop minestrone soup cauldron some ten feet away!

Far right activist Robinson, now in full view with nunchaku stretched out horizontally in front of him, runs screaming towards the gathered backbenchers, martial arts weapon flailing as they beat a panicked retreat behind upturned tables and while May's attention is distracted and her back is turned by the arrival of SCYL, bloodied eared Corbyn, missing front teeth Bercow, glass-eye Brown and bloody nosed Brummie Basher Watson combine to body slam her to the floor, piling on top of one another in true football celebration style and then rising, with two at either end, they lift her up by her arms and legs and start crab-walking her semi-conscious, L. K. Bennett tweed jacketed and Vivienne Westwood Anglomania Kung Fu tapered wool pants-clad body towards the dining hall's historic, stained glass windows that overlook the River Thames, passing a tomato-faced Dennis 'the Menace' Skinner MP, the 'Bolsover Bulldog', who is straining to push a fully laden shimmy-wheeled wooden trolley of House of Commons memorabilia, closely followed by his assistant, 'Billionaire Bludgeoner' Lloyd Russell-Moyle MP.

'Roll up! Roll up! Come and get it! House of Commons tea towels, Union Jack teacup and saucers and mantel-piece flags! *Dodgy Dave* face masks and a second-hand, gilded silver ceremonial mace!' Skinner shouts, gesturing towards a staggering, sweat-drenched Russell-Moyle, who is struggling to carry the House of Commons five-foot, glittering gold-coloured royal mace in both arms. 'And last but not least, the number one bestselling A-five pamphlet, *Standing Order Number Forty Three!*' Skinner breathlessly bellows as they inch their way through the caterwauling crowd.

Gathering momentum, Corbyn and crew side step through the ensuing melee, as chanting, fist-pumping MPs – some sat atop other's shoulders – separate to make way, before an unexpected straight arm with a clenched fist attached shoots out to impact the side of Brown's face, *WHALLOP!* popping out his glass eye and sending it spinning, ironically and quite unexpectedly, into the open mouth of a grimacing, gobstopper gasping, beetroot Blair, who is now stood coughing as he chokes and clutches at his throat, collapsing to the floor once again.

'Hammond, you miserable, lank-haired fucker!' Brown shouts up from the polished deck, where he's laid out, somewhat dazed, as the chancellor takes a step back in his goth-style black buckled boots and *Matrix* black leather trench coat, ready to use Brown's head for penalty kick practise.

'Kiss my hairy bean bag, Brown!' Hammond spits, just as a whittled table leg bloodily erupts out of his chest, *Alien*-style, impaling him mid-swing as Nicola Sturgeon's grinning Peyton Place appears next to his.

'Now that's what I call pushing your policies through,' the Scottish First Minister says, and kisses the Chancellor on the cheek a moment before he drops. 'Us Scots need to stick together, Gordon,' she winks, folding away her Girl Guides pocket penknife and wiping her bloodied hands across her hips, before lunging back into the churning throng.

Labour and Conservative, and Liberal Democrat and SNP, and Independent and DUP MPs, now roughly split and gathered into gangs of Remoaners and Brexiteers, are facing off, with some swinging on the chandeliers like crazed, drunken chimpanzees, while Dominic Raab MP stands centre ground between the opposing factions, lunch napkin tucked into his shirt collar, supported by Caroline Lucas MP, the solitary Green Party Member of Parliament, as they endeavour to keep both groups at bay with outstretched arms.

'Thanks for your help, Ms Lucas,' Raab says above the racket, putting his military training to good use as he tries to restore order.

'Don't mention it, Mr Rub,' Lucas replies.

'Sorry, but it's Raab!'

'I know, Mr Rub, don't mention it!' Lucas says again, raising her voice.

'It's Raab, Ms Lucas!'

'Mr Rub, I know who you are! Please stop repeating your name when we really do have more pressing issues!'

'It's just too noisy in here, that's why you can't hear me properly.'

'It's *Rub*, isn't it? Like one of our policies, to make a bark rubbing from a tree!'

'No, it's *Raa*- oh, never mind! Just stand your ground while I try and talk some sense into these nut fucks.'

'OK, Mr Rub.'

'Gentlemen, ladies, please put down your dining room crockery and table furniture and return to your seats before your lunches get cold. We must remain calm and talk this through.'

'Mind your own business, Rub!' an MP shouts out, as others start jeering him.

'Yeah, piss off back to your barracks and your Rad's Army!'

'Bye-bye, Raby, Raby *goodbye!'*

'It's actually Raab,' Raab corrected, 'not Rub, Rad or Raby!'

'Bye-bye, Raby, *don't make me cry!'*

'Leave means leave, Rub!'

'Rub-a-dub-dub, you're tryin' to rob us, Rub!' a lone voice shouts above the hubbub.

'It's *Raab,* and I'm actually on your side!' Raab protests.

'Keep your nose out, Rub, before we rub your nose in it!'

'It's *Raab*, not Rab or Reb, or Rib or Rob, or even Rub, but *Raab*, like a lion's roar, but with an A – Rah!' Raab vociferates, finally losing his rag. 'Try singing it like a nursery rhyme, "Rah, Rah *black sheep, have you any wool?"* A sort of back of the throat, guttural sound, *ahhhh*, very similar to gargling with hot saltwater, in fact. Just throw your head back and relax your throat, *ahhhh*, but with an R at the beginning, as in Rahhh!'

'You are really Raabing everyone up the wrong way,' a voice shouts, as Raab shrugs his shoulders and, in the interests of self-preservation, instinctively retreats, grabbing Lucas and diving for cover as the room erupts with chairs and table legs, and plates and cups and saucers, and food and drink flying through the air in all directions, like a dozen university mortarboard celebrations rolled into one, as numerous psycho diners fly past screaming, *'ARRRRGH!'*

'No, for pity's sake, and once and for all, it's *Rahhhh*, not *arrrrgh*! My name is *RAAB!'* he yells, a bulging

M1-sized jugular vein running the length of his reddening neck, as an incoming spinning table leg missile hits him square in the chest, dislodging his lunch napkin! *'ARRRRGH!'* he cries, crumpling to the floor.

'I thought you said it was Raab, with an R, not *Arrrrgh* but *Raaaaaa?'* Lucas says, kneeling down to gently raise a semi-conscious Raab up into her lap.

'Oh, bugger and damnation,' he moans, 'I think I've broken my ribs!'

'You've broken your rabs?' Lucas asks, voice raised over the din.

'Oh, sod it, yes! Close enough, and I've also got indigestion and bloody heartburn now as well,' Raab moans, looking up at Lucas with half lidded eyes. 'I think I've got some Rennie, if that would help?' Lucas offers, cradling him as she starts to rock him to sleep and sings, *'Rock-a-bye,* Raby, *on the treetop, When the wind blows, the cradle will rock...'*

On the other side of the dining hall, a blowing, buggered Bercow is straining to bring up the slack, as he struggles to carry May's blue suede shoe-encased feet. For their part, Corbyn and Watson offer encouragement by advising him to, 'Put your back into it, you pontificating pussy!'

Meanwhile, Brown, still dizzy from Hammond's punch and shocked at his subsequent swift demise, has come to his senses enough to roll over onto all fours and crawl towards blue-faced Blair. 'Don't cry for me, *Granita!*' he croons, dripping tears of laughter onto Blair's angelic, stilton-coloured features. 'An eye for an eye, eh, Tony?' he whispers, affectionately tapping his former leader on the cheek and rising to stand, he stomps on Blair's stomach, folding him upwards in half, causing Blair to spit out his glass eye with a *WHOOSH!* sending it flying across the dining hall into a plate of food counter custard cream cakes.

PLOP!

Having finally arrived at the stained glass windows overlooking the Thames, Corbyn, Watson and Bercow are literally in full swing, as May gains ever increasing height and momentum, while across the hall, the spinning shepherd's crook-wielding Archbishop of Canterbury trades blows with Tommy Robinson, like a kayak canoeing Jedi Knight Kung Fu master, defending himself against Robinson's lightning-fast whirling nunchaku.

'I christen this ship, Queen Theresa! May God bless her and all who sail in her!' a breathless Bercow proclaims, giggling as May is swung backwards and forwards like a swaying windblown hammock.

It's one for the money, two for the show, three to get ready, now go, Prime Minister, go!' Watson warbles.

'So, today we're going to see the first airborne prime minister thrown through the... perpendicular gothic revival stained glass window,' Bercow announces, laughing as he recalls the BBC children's television series *Play School.*

'Mayday! Mayday! Abandon ship!' Corbyn shouts at the top of his voice, and with one final heave-ho,

May is finally thrown sideways through the stained glass windows with such force that a passing tourist, sitting on the upper deck of an open-topped double decker London tour bus on Westminster Bridge, sees what looks like a flailing, wailing mannequin flying ragdoll-like into the river with a loud *'ARRRRGH!'* and an even louder *SPLASH!*

'God, I thought she'd never fuck off!' a grinning Corbyn exclaims, rubbing his blood-encrusted ear as Bercow and Watson high five, and turning his attention back towards the canteen, he quickly spots a familiar face in the distance, pummelling Farage against the serving hatch wall with Galloway on his back, wrapped around his neck like a human ruck-sack. 'Oh shit, it's Bovver Boot Boris!' he exhales dramatically. 'One down, one to go.'

All three start unscrewing table legs as Farage, pummelled almost to a pulp by Boris, retaliates desperately with a picture-perfect uppercut, bouncing the back of Boris's blond thatched bonce off Galloway's nose with an audible crunch, as the bloodied, broken-nosed Scot unwraps himself and starts highland jigging with a yelp, while Boris staggers sideways before slumping face down into plated custard cream cakes.

'Blond-haired bastard!' Farage yells, wincing from the beating he's just endured as Galloway nods, holding a blood-soaked, House of Commons logo-embossed white tea towel to his nose as they both look over at Tommy Robinson, now worryingly overwhelmed and surrounded, and in urgent response they quickly grab a variety of kitchen utensils and scream in unison, *'Once more unto the breach, dear friends!'* as they vault over the food counter, rolling pin, soup ladle and cauldron lids in hand.

Boris, meanwhile, opens his eyes, blinking whipped cream-covered, snowflake eyelashes and, rising upwards, separates his suctioned face from the selection of cream cakes with a *SSHLUP*, spitting out a large, eye-like marble with disgust onto the floor, and after wiping his mouth with a cufflinked sleeve, he leaps over the food counter, gazelle-like, moving quickly to penalty kick Galloway in the bagpipes from behind. 'Back of the net!' he cries, fist pumping in celebration as Galloway falls to the floor with an

'*OOOOWWWHH!*' and catching a Cameron-thrown table leg mid-air, Boris then proceeds to close the gap on Farage, unaware that Corbyn, Watson and Bercow, now rejoined by blusher-cheeked Brown, have already negotiated the collapsed and upturned tables and scattered chairs chicane, and are marching towards him with malicious intent.

'Ah, Mr Brexit,' Remain goalkeeper Oliver Letwin MP says, facing off against Farage and launching an over the top haymaker.

'Oliver, my dear,' Farage retorts, blocking Letwin's blow with perfect *X Factor* crossed arms before hitting Mr Amendment for six, bouncing him off tables like a pond-skimming stone. 'Consider yourself part of the furniture!' he shouts. 'Oh, and Oliver, I presume you don't want any more?' he grins, picking up his pastry pin and metal lid on the way to joining Robinson and teary-eyed Galloway, still stood clutching his family jewels, and three unknown little old ladies wearing *LEAVE MEANS LEAVE!* t-shirts.

Almost immediately, and upon Farage's command, they all start frantically forming a Billy Smart's Circus human triangle, with Farage, Robinson and Galloway at the base, catering weapons in hand, supporting two little old ladies above, who in turn are supporting one little old lady at the top, stood in a defensive line, making their few in number appear as big and thereby as threatening to the opposition as possible, as Robinson, Farage and Galloway are immediately put to work defending themselves against a jousting Archbishop, as well as numerous Labour and Conservative back-benchers and stretchered out heavyweight radio presenter Nick Ferrari substitutes, James O'Brien and Nick Abbot, aka *Doom and Gloom*, with indiscriminate elbows and fist-gripped weapons and cauldron lid shields, while kicking out like a John Cleese in *Fawlty Towers* dance troupe tribute act doing the cancan, until notorious busybody Anna Soubry MP steps forward, backed up by stern-faced Armageddon twins Doom and Gloom, shaking her head and wagging a pointed finger at the three acrobatic old ladies. 'Now stop this at once and come down from there, for goodness' sake,' she demands, hands now on hips. 'You should all be ashamed of yourselves! We are not leaving anything.

We're going to have a second referendum and *that's* final! Now, get down!'

'Fuck off back to Sherwood Forest, Maid Marian!' the little old lady at the pinnacle of the triangle heckles from up high. 'We're fucking off, and that's fucking final!'

But as luck would have it, and with perfect timing, Ann Widdecombe MEP appears as if by magic, wearing a lovely Laura Ashley floral print dress with matching handbag, wading into the circus like a bull in a china shop, and immediately dispatches Soubry with a perfect jaw-crunching right, knocking her into the middle of next week. 'It seems some crunts need *Nanny McPheeing!*' she cries, going berserk with a primal *'ARRRGH!*' as Doom and Gloom step forward, fists clenched and jaws twitching, ready to *'GOWE!*' Widdecombe giving them a *'WANT SOME?*' look and screams, 'Let's change the bloody record, shall we!' before landing stereo uppercuts in a blistering, figure of eight double handbag swing, *BOOF-BOOF!*'... a bowling ball taking out all ten pins, twice! STRIKE ONE! STRIKE TWO! Leaving *Bill and Ben the*

Flower Pot Men rolling around on top of each other and groaning, *'Flopolloppollop!'*

Farage is spurred on chortling with Robinson and Galloway in support, as they push forwards at such a pace that they spontaneously catapult the three little old ladies through the air and into the enemy camp, like stray cannonballs at the Battle of Waterloo!

'Fuck me!' exclaims a gawping Galloway, his attention caught by the three sugar gliding possum, drawers flapping *Flying Brexiteers*, as Farage pushes him over onto the floor and, grabbing him by the ankles, spins him around three times, hammer throwing him, Geoff Capes-style, into the baying mob.

'No problem, George!' Farage shouts, as Galloway disappears into the thick of it with an *'ARRRRGH!'*

Boris, on the other hand, has stepped back to avoid 'wild cat' Widdecombe, the 'Bath Bashing Somerset Slayer,' and, clutching his table leg, he focusses his attention on the four amigos closing in on his left flank and resigned to the futility of his position, he lays down his weapon and lifts up a one-legged circular table off the floor, rolling it towards them while crouch-crawl hiding behind it.

Then suddenly, out of the blue, or more accurately, out of the brown, a sodden, muddy, dishevelled and dripping zombie swamp creature appears in the dining hall entrance, and even by zombie swamp creature standards, this one looks pissed off!

'Ah, Theresa, I honestly thought you'd fucked off,' Ken Clarke says, passing the PM on his way out of the bloodied lunch arena, cigar in hand.

'Shut it, piss head!' May snaps, and with a swift right hook, sends him crashing to the canvass.

When May left earlier, albeit somewhat unexpectedly, things were hotting up but now the dining hall has turned into a bloody, burning, hell on earth smoking war zone.

'I'm a bitch, I'm a bitch, oh, the bitch is back,' she sings to herself, gently robot swaying as she surveys

the battleground, *'Stone cold sober, as a matter of fact! I can bitch, I can bitch, 'cause I'm better than you, It's the way that I move, the things that I do, oh!'* she snickers. 'Thought they'd got rid of me, did they? Well, not yet. Not *fucking* yet!' she snarls under her breath, and bending down, she unfastens Clarke's trouser belt buckle and yanks the leather strap free of his trousers, spinning him like a fat pork sausage being turned in a frying pan as he rolls off, cigar smoke trailing, towards the exit! 'The House! The House! My kingdom for the House!' she screams, re-entering the fray with Clarke's leather belt rotating above her head.

'Stone the crows!' a shocked Watson exclaims, mouth open catching flies, as he suddenly halts and stops everyone else in their tracks. 'Fucking hell! No way – no fucking way!'

'What is it, Basher?' Corbyn enquires.

'You're not going to believe this!'

'What?'

'You are *not* going to fucking believe this!'

'Fucking what?! What is it?!'

'Fucking fucketty fuck!'

'What the fuck is it, what? Nicola Sturgeon is expecting Tony Blair's love child?'

'What?'

'Oh, do fuck off, Jeremy, you black eyepatch prick!'

'Well, fucking what, then?' Corbyn asks again, exasperated.

'TM is bloody back!' Watson answers.

'Trade mark you mean?'

'What? No! How can a trade mark come back?'

'Text message then!?'

'Are you clinically insane?!'

'Trevor McDonald?'

'Oh, fuck off and die, granddad!'

'Transcendental meditation?'

'I'm actually losing the will to live.'

'Taj Mahal? Time Machine? What the bloody hell are you saying, Basher?'

'The fucking Queen Bitch is back!'

'Margaret Fucking Thatcher?'

'Oh, for fuck's sake!'

'What then? Fucking spit it out!'

'Fucking May's back!'

'The Queen guitarist?' Corbyn asks, totally bewildered.

'No, you fucking idiot!'

'I don't understand! What the fuck are you talking about?'

'Do you give up?'

'Yes, *I GIVE UP!*' Corbyn shouts!

'Are you absolutely sure?'

'JUST FUCKING TELL ME!'

'OK, are you ready? May's back. Fucking *THERESA MAY!* Remember her? She is fucking back. *THERESA MAY IS FUCKING BACK!* Get it? Got it? Good!'

'Are you telling me that the Prime Minister, Theresa May, is back? The queen bitch, who we hoiked through a stained-glass window into the fucking Thames, is back? Is that what you are fucking telling me, Basher?'

'Yes, that is what I am telling you, Jeremy. That's what I'm FUCKING TELLING YOU EXACTLY!' Basher screams welling up, holding onto Corbyn's jacket lapels with white-knuckled fists.

'Hell's fucking holy mackerel bastard bells!'

'And flippin' heck, guess what? She doesn't look all that chuffed!'

'No shit, Sherlock!' shocked Corbyn says, furrow-browed.

'In fact, you might say she's somewhat miffed, possibly even really annoyed!' Basher adds, releasing his grip as Brown starts impersonating Shakin' Stevens.

'She's the bloody Terminator!' Corbyn says, putting a clenched fist to his mouth and biting on it. 'The EU's invigilator!'

'You mean the Brexit Hater!' Basher replies, teeth wobbling.

'She's total mayhem!' Brown blurts between quivering lips.

'She's fucking indestructible!' Corbyn laments. 'She's Captain bloody Scarlett!'

'Or the Mysterons' mischief maker!' Basher quips.

'Total malfunction!' Brown cries. 'I'm a teapot, I'm a teapot, I'm a fucking teapot!'

'Calm yourself, Gordon for fuck's sake!' Corbyn snaps. 'If we lose it now, we'll never get rid of her!'

'She's a bloody witch, that's what she is,' Brown screams, eye the size of a dinner plate. 'She's cursed and we're doomed. We're all FUCKING DOOMED!'

SLAP!

'Whoa, what the fuck?' Basher cries.

'Hello chaps,' a noodle-encrusted-faced, blood-stained, creased white-shirted Tony Blair says, shaking his right hand with a wince, after slapping Brown across the face. 'Is this a private party, or can anyone join in?'

'What the bloody hell was that for?' Brown bleats, holding his cheek.

'Sorry, Gordon, force of habit,' Blair explains. 'I thought it might help!'

'No problem, Tony,' Brown replies, as Blair supports him by the elbow.

'Feeling better?'

'Yes, thanks, Tony, I needed that.'

'So did I,' Blair admits, tapping his stomach. 'Oh, by the way, I've brought a friend. Alistair are you ready?'

'Just let me finish tying my shoelace and I'm there,' a familiar voice says. 'Hello Gordon.'

'Alastair!'

'I hear you pricks need some help getting rid of the witch from Maidenhead – the cat with nine lives,' Blair's former Director of Communications Alastair Campbell says with a smile, standing.

'Too bloody right!' Corbyn replies.

'Tony?' Campbell says, stepping back.

'Hold up, Mr Meatballs, why don't you step up to the plate for once?' Basher asks accusingly.

'Why own a dog and bark yourself?' Campbell smirks, as Basher eyeballs him.

'OK, let's get organised,' Blair says, stepping forward to take charge. 'Jezza, you're our defence, with Gordon and Bercow in support.'

'Whoa, wait a minute!' Corbyn objects. 'What's your game, matey? I'm in charge now!' he growls, gnashing his bared teeth.

'Be careful what you wish for, Jezza!' Blair advises.

'You had your chance, and you fucked it up good and proper!'

'Don't say anything you'll regret Corbyn!' Blair warns him between tight lips!

'You've got no skin in this game, matey, so piss off back to your coal mine, unless you want some that is, Queensbury Rules-style!' Corbyn snarls, assuming the fists raised stance, staring down Blair who stares right back at Corbyn, who stares back at Blair, who stares back at Corbyn, who stares back at Blair, who stares back at Corbyn, who stares back at Blair. Bercow checks his waistcoat pocket watch, as Blair stares back at Corbyn, who stares back at Blair, who stares back at Corbyn, who stares back at Blair, who blinks at Corbyn, who stares back at Blair, who averts his gaze and admires his shoes.

'OK, fair cop! It's all yours, Captain!' Blair concedes, bowing out and stepping back, doffs his hat as Corbyn drops his hands and takes centre stage.

'Friends, Londoners, countrymen, lend me an ear plaster, if you have one!' Corbyn begins his rallying cry. 'I come to bury May, not to praise her! Never in the field of Parliamentary conflict has so much been owed by so few to so many! This gathered band of brothers, for he today that sheds his blood with me shall be my brother, as long as he has a tin of plasters with him! Brave and courageous men of this land of hope and glory, of the United Kingdom of Great Britain and Northern Island, of great British grit, who proudly live and would die for their Queen and country with honour, England expects that every man will do his duty for Prince Harry and Saint George, to fight and stop Brexit and have a second referendum day!' he proclaims vigorously, as the troops applaud and cheer.

Gordon Brown's eye glistens as, mouth quivering, he moves to hug Corbyn and starts to sob!

'Kismet, Brownie,' Corbyn whispers.

'The king is dead, long live the king!' Bercow pronounces.

'Great speech, Horatio!' Blair says, applauding Corbyn.

'OK, Gordon, it's alright, shush. Everything is going to be fine,' Corbyn says, gently directing Brown by his elbow back to Blair's bosom and pulling out of his inside jacket pocket and putting on his black Leninist cap, he grabs a chair on which to stand. 'Ahoy, me hearties! Avast ye, me crew of black-hearted pirates! It'll be all hands on deck, with Campbell, Brown and Bercow in defence, and Basher, Blair and me, Captain Corbyn, in attack! So, batten down the hatches and prepare to board the enemy ship! Fight hard and true, and if this skirmish win we do, then shiver me timbers, we'll splice the main brace and I'll cross your palms with silver! Draw your table legs and prepare to fight! Yo-ho-ho and a bottle of rum, put May in leg irons to walk the plank, and the mandolin we'll strum all the way to the bank! Are ye ready?' Corbyn calls out rallying his troops, raising his table leg scabbard above his head. 'I said, are ye ready?'

'Aye aye, Captain!' the Labour men shout in unison, scabbard's held aloft.

Meanwhile, May has spotted Corbyn and crew in the distance, and has locked onto them like a missile defence system and with a piercing scream that only bats could hear, she cracks her leather belt whip in true Rawhide style and launches at them, sprinting headfirst in full nuclear weapons strike mode. Unfortunately, however, May's attention is distance-focussed and thereby she is unaware that Boris's rolling table will, at any moment, block her warpath. While Boris, renowned for his intuitive nature and keen sense of timing, is also completely oblivious to this fact, as May's head, shoulders and arms suddenly smash through the table that he is rolling, with a splintering *CRACK*!

'Fuck me!' Boris exclaims, falling backwards, as a damp patch instantly appears across his crotch.

'With pleasure, you jaywalking twat!' May spits, grabbing his golden mop and repeatedly bashing his blonde bouffant barnet bonce into the varnished wood. 'NEVER... EVER... VOTE... AGAINST... ME... AGAIN... YOU... MODEL... BUS... BUILDING... BASTARD!' she screams, starting to feel herself slowly turning, trapped in the middle of the table, as the room begins to rotate, forcing her to relinquish her grip on Boris's thatch, only to catch a revolving glimpse of Blair, Campbell, Watson, Brown, Corbyn and Bercow's ecstatic faces as she rolls past them at ever increasing speed.

'I thought you'd fucked off!' Corbyn shouts over the cacophony of cackles and curses.

'Join the bleedin' queue!' May shouts back, as Watson, Blair and Campbell, now joined by bruised-bonce Boris, all rush to push against the vertical table's edge with one final joint effort.

'Et tu, Boris, then fall Theresa!' May cries, as she rotates on her way towards the dining hall exit, looking like she's being eaten by some sort of giant killer chocolate digestive biscuit. '*ARRRRGH*!' she screams, as she accelerates, rolling off out of sight.

The *Dragged Through a Ditch and Then Through a Hedge Backwards Club* members, Brown, Bercow and Boris, stand hands on hips, grinning, while Blair,

Campbell, Corbyn and Watson embrace one another, back slapping in their torn battle fatigues, and Bercow is lifted up to sit astride Corbyn's shoulders.

Raising his clenched-fisted arm in ecstatic jubilation, the speaker cries out, 'ORDER! ORDER! WE'VE JUST RESTORED BLOODY ORDER!' punching the air like he's just scored the winning goal in the FA Cup final while Blair works the room, shaking hands and smiling like sun-kissed treacle, thanking everyone for their loyal support.

Unfortunately, such joyous occasions seldom last, especially in politics, and sure enough this was one of them, as an out of sight and therefore out of mind, but no less perfectly aimed rolling pin warhead spins silently through the air, slamming straight into the back of Bercow's loaf of bread, simultaneously knocking him out and off Corbyn's shoulders straight onto the floor with a *SMACK*!

'Did somebody say *ORDER?*' a battered, grinning, sweaty, wide-eyed Farage asks, cauldron lid in hand as he suddenly appears before the shell-shocked group. 'Because mine's a fucking PINT!' he exclaims, picking up his wooden pastry weapon from next to prostrate Bercow.

'Bloody good shot, though,' Corbyn acknowledges, voice wavering again.

'Not really, granddad, I was aiming for you!' Farage admits, tapping the rolling pin on Corbyn's shoulders, as if he was knighting him.

'Ah, I see. Oh well, best be getting on, then,' Corbyn replies meekly and, grabbing Basher Watson by the scruff of the neck, staggers off.

'Silence is golden, But my eyes still see, Silence is golden, golden, But my eyes still see...' Farage sings down at Bercow. 'You know, if push comes to shove, he could always apply to be the new House of Commons short order cook! *Scramble! Chocks away!'* Farage declares, saluting the dumbfounded posse with his rolling pin and, cauldron lid in hand, returns to the front line, leaving Blair, Brown, Campbell and Boris glued to the spot, gawping like goldfish.

'Well, one thing's for sure,' Blair says above the racket, breaking the chummy silence, while still focussed, along with everyone else, on the groaning Bercow laid out flat as a pancake, 'with cold-blooded instincts like that, Farage deserves to be Prime Minister!' and turning to survey the dining hall devastation, he sets off to return to his table and collect his suit jacket when, through pure bad luck and perfectly bad timing, he slips on a glass marble that sends him skywards. *'WHOA!'* he wails, landing on his back on top of an adjacent table... SLAM! and with an audible moan, rolls off the table straight into the lap of Ann 'Whoop Ass' Widdecombe, who is sat on her tea break, enjoying a deliciously refreshing English bone china cup of Yorkshire Tea, held with the saucer at chest height.

Unfazed by this extraordinary turn of events, she looks down at the concussed Blair languishing face down in her lap, and leisurely finishes her tea before placing the teacup back on its saucer and then places the teacup and saucer back on the table. 'Tony, we simply *must* stop meeting like this,' she says sarcastically, clutching her handbag and knees Blair in his

Wendi Murdoch Device as she rises, letting him drop to the floor with a *SMACK*! 'Oh dear, how unfortunate! Is there a doctor in the House?' she asks the room, seriously concerned for Blair's welfare.

'May I be of service?' enquires enthusiastic, smiling school prefect Jeremy Hunt, rushing over to give mouth to mouth.

'Oh, look, it's Hunt the Hunt!' exclaims Widdecombe.

'Ha-ha-ha! Hello Ann,' Hunt smiles sweetly. 'Could I suggest McDonald's? That's where most doctors work nowadays, after I ripped the guts out of the NHS!'

'Well, that's another fine mess you've got the NHS into, so you'd better bugger off there sharpish then, hadn't you, and get help!' Widdecombe replies sternly.

'Please, Ann, I just want to help. Let's not argue like two snarling, mangy, rabid foxes at fisticuffs over disputed territory, deep in the Berkshire countryside. Let's work together as one and help poor Tony.'

'You really are on crack aren't you, Mr Runt? Have you been raiding the NHS county hospital medicine cabinet? No wonder there's a shortage of bloody drugs, let alone bloody doctors!'

'Please, Ann, let's all work together as a team, unselfishly, like doctors and nurses curing the sick and healing the wounded, come on!' he says, puppy-dog eyes pleading!

'If only I had a Bedlam hospital bedpan, I'd hit you over the head with it, but I'll tell you what, rather than squabble like your two feline friends, let's play WTP, or *What's the Phrase?* Whoever wins decides who helps Tony.'

'Super!'

'OK, Mr Hunt, this is your impossible mission. Are you ready to accept it?'

'Yes! Oh yes, I am!' Hunt replies enthusiastically.

'OK, I'll go first.'

'OK, Ann, great idea.'

'OK! Nine-letter phrase beginning with an *I*, made up of one letter *I* and then a two-letter word, followed by a one-letter vowel and finally a five-letter word, used by an individual to describe themselves in a positive light. Are you ready?'

'How exciting!' Hunt says, face lit up, bright-eyed and hands repeatedly clapping together like a manic orchestral cymbalist on speed. 'Right, yes, let's bloody go for it!'

'Don't forget, it is a four-word phrase with a total of nine letters.'

'OK, a four-word phrase used by someone to describe themselves in a positive light, made up of nine letters starting with an *I*. OK, right then, let me think, OK, erm, oh dear, erm, right, erm, first letter was *I*, yes, OK, erm, *I*, first letter, OK, *I*, erm, spy, right, erm, so, *I spy*, erm, OK, *with my*, erm, *with*, erm, goodness me, *with my little eye*. Yes, there you have it. *I spy with my little eye!* Perfect!'

'That's nineteen letters, Jeremy,' Widdecombe points out, looking at Hunt in disbelief.

'Ah yes, right, oh dear!'

'Try again, Jeremy. Second time lucky, and don't rush, just take your time. In fact, imagine you are a patient on an NHS waiting list, or sat in A and E! You've got all the time in the world.'

'OK, great, Ann, marvellous! Right, erm, put your thinking cap on, Jeremy! OK, erm, right, first letter *I* and second word am, so, erm, *I am*, OK, good, erm, right, OK, yes, I think, yes, I think I've got it, yes, perfect! It's *I am what I am!*' he beams.

'Well, we all know that, Jeremy, but unfortunately that's ten letters. Four words, yes, but ten letters! You obviously failed your maths GCSE.'

'Oh fiddlesticks!'

'Do you want to phone a friend, Jeremy?'

'Oh, could I, Ann? That would be wonderful?'

"You don't have any friends, Jeremy.'

'Oh yes, of course! Oh dear! Well, just let me think for a moment, erm, right, oh dear, goodness me, erm, sorry, I seem to be really and truly flummoxed, so I guess I'll give up.'

'Good guess, but only seven letters, so you're wrong again.'

'Sorry?'

'Apology accepted, but "I give up" is not correct.'

'Ah, I didn't actually mean that, I meant, well, never mind! Oh dear, I'm somewhat stuck then, aren't I?' he says disappointedly.

'Don't worry, Jeremy, let me help you.'

'Oh, bless you, Ann!'

'Please repeat after me, putting the letters into complete words and saying them out loud. OK?'

'OK!'

'Ready?'

'Yes, ready when you are.'

'OK, first word is I.'

'OK, right, yes, I.'

'*A-M*... am.'

'Am.'

'*A*.'

'A.'

'C-R-U-N-T... Crunt.'

'Crunt.'

'I... am... a... crunt.'

'I am a crunt! ... I am a crunt?' Hunt asks, eyebrows elevated in a perfect impersonation of a bewildered Stan Laurel.

'You said it!' Widdecombe replies, as she sends Hunt cross-eyed to the floor with a perfect handbag between the legs 'nutcracker!'

'*OOOOWWWWHH!*'

'Nurse, I said remove his TESTICLES!' she shouts out, laughing as she steps past Hunt and over a drooling Blair, now sound asleep on the floor and sucking his thumb while snoring, before unexpectedly bumping into the back of bouffant Boris. 'Oi, Boris, you wanker, time to face the fucking music!' she growls, handbag at the ready as he slowly turns around, engaging her with a disarmingly intense stare.

'I think you mean my son,' Michael Fabricant MP replies with a resolute smile, before realigning his coiffure and striding past a thunderstruck Widdecombe, and then carefully tiptoeing over Blair and Hunt to disappear into the fractious fracas.

Flabbergasted and mouth agape in shock as she tries to fully compute the recently imputed data, Widdecombe spots a fellow soldier at arms and, regaining her focus, scurries over to dripping-faced Farage, who is stood bent over, hands on knees, taking a well-earned rest with his rolling pin and cauldron lid at his feet.

'Nigel! Nigel, are you alright?' she asks, genuinely concerned.

'Ann, oh thank the Lords, yes, yes, I'm fine,' he says, panting, 'just trying to catch my breath. I wondered where the hell you'd got to!'

'Well, here I am, Nigel, rocking and rolling as per usual.'

'You look somewhat pale, though, Ann. Are you sure you're OK?'

'Oh yes, just a little fatigued, I suppose. That's all.'

There Is Only Now

'Bloody hell, join the club! I'm absolutely cream crackered!'

'Still, it's better to stand up straight, I would suggest. It allows better oxygenation of the blood, and therefore a quicker recovery time.'

'Good idea! Now I understand why we're jaw-jaw not war-war!' he chuckles, wiping the sweat from his brow and sweeping his hair back as he stands.

'The pen is mightier than the Tsar Bomba thermonuclear weapon, after all.'

'You can say that again.'

'Erm, no thanks!'

'Ann,' he says softly, reaching out to hold her hand.

'What is it?'

'You do know that I love you, don't you?' he says, gently squeezing her fingers while she stares back at

— 101 —

him with smiling eyes, pupils dilating. 'Always have and always will.'

'I know, Nigel,' she whispers, delicately cupping his sweaty cheek with her free hand and, returning his affectionate gesture, giving him the faintest of winks, 'I know.'

Widdecombe turns and heads off towards the exit, just as a hospital gown-attired, flip flop wearing, saline drip bag attached IV stand on wheels-pushing John Prescott appears in the dining hall entrance.

'Ah, Ms Widdecombe, I presume,' Prescott greets the departing MEP.

'Hello John, how are you?' she asks.

'Fucked, in a word!'

'Yes, I can see.'

'Heard about all the commotion, though, and got down here as quickly as I could. Am I too late?'

'No, we're just about to start the second half actually, with us *Brexiteers* trouncing the *Remoaners* by a distance, but there are still a few pockets of resistance, so I'm just off to spend a penny and then I'll be back, but you'll find Hunt 'the Crunt' clutching his P and Ts over there, lying next to thumb-sucking, baby-drooling Blair, and stretchered out substitutions aside, the rest of the mobocrasy gang are still sorting out their differences, but who'd have thought that Brexit constituency MPs would vote to stop Brexit, eh, John? What a kick in the nuts for their constituents! Bloody turncoat traitors.'

'It's called *fraudmocracy*, Ann, and we either accept it or fight to change it!' Prescott says with a look of resignation.

'Anyway, as a matter of interest and on a more personal note,' Widdecombe lowers her voice as she looks right and then left, and right again, moving closer to Prezza, 'and for your ears only, I'm sure I overheard Corbyn, Brown and crew joking about the fact that years ago, you used to work as a waiter on a ferry!'

Prescott looks shocked, as he starts to boil. 'WHAT?' he yells, bloodshot eyes about to pop, as his face impersonates a traffic light on STOP!

'Oh yes, they were laughing so hard, they were literally pissing themselves!'

'Fucking backstabbing bastards!' Prescott roars and, lifting up his hospital smock with his free hand, he starts sprinting *flip-flop-flip-flop-flip-flop* towards the front line, his wheel-mounted drip stand clattering behind him as he charges into battle with a deafening, *'ARRRRGH!'*

'Enjoy,' Widdecombe smiles, 'I'll be back in a jiffy!'

Clutching her handbag, she turns to leave the dining hall, only to find her path blocked by a navy blue tracksuit and white trainers-clad, crown-wearing, handbag-carrying little old lady.

'Is one shooting orf, then?' HRH Queen Elizabeth II asks Widdecombe, as the latter hastily curtsies.

'Your majesty! I just need to powder my nose,' Widdecombe splutters nervously, bowing her head.

'Well, giddy-up! One needs to find the cheeky buggers who nicked one's ceremonial golden mace, before the lunatics really do take over the bloody asylum.'

'Yes, ma'am!' Widdecombe replies, rising.

'Oh, and Ms Widdecombe,' HRH adds, eyes gleaming.

'Yes, ma'am?'

'If one is going to get these crunts, it's handbags at the ready, handbags at the ready!'

Mr Richard

Dogs and cats and goldfish, too; even a slippery snake that sleeps in the loo, always wet in the morning from the night before, as I try to remember not to flush! Oh, and a rhinoceros in the back garden called Mr Richard. Our home really is a sort of private zoo, but I am no Dr Dolittle, although ironically, I don't do that much as I leave it all to my wife, who leaves it to the cleaner to mop up the wee and vac up the poo!

Until that midweek morning early, when I found Mr Richard floating upside down in our outdoor pool, inflated swimming bands-wearing, Belisha beacon legs stuck up vertically straight out of the water, pointing skywards; miniature orange bulbous-leafed palm trees glistening in the sunlight.

I walk through into our murky, English oak-panelled dining room at first light and stand frowning, condensed water vapour rising from my saucer-held first cup of tea of the day, perplexed by the absence of the external garden security lighting which normally dimly illuminates the room and its original, pride of place, Glenn D. Webster abstract artwork from beneath the base of the drawn vintage velvet curtains. Elevating my right arm, I grip the delicate teacup handle between the thumb and index finger of my right hand and, raising the cup to my mouth, I take a sip of the delicious oil of bergamot-infused hot liquid, fragrant citrus invading my nostrils as I replace the cup in the saucer, inhaling deeply and securing it in my left hand. Walking over to the far wall, where fixed at shoulder-height is a two gang grid modular plate, I single-handedly flick the external garden security light switch up and down and up and down, with the thumb and index finger of my right hand, and then finally up again, focussing with each movement on the bottom of the curtains seeing that they remain unlit. Flicking the adjacent second switch upwards into the off position, I turn off the outdoor pool lighting. Half turning, I grip the cord pull weight and draw the curtains, as sparkling early morning sunlight invades the caliginous room and, unlocking and opening the garden doors, I step out onto our recently extended south-facing patio, instantly dropping my white bone china teacup and saucer in shock, Earl Grey tea splashing against handmade, antique Spanish terracotta tiles, sunlit steaming.

Porcelain cup and saucer explode into innumerable jigsaw puzzle piece fragments, and I'm sprinting towards the pool across dew-damp, moss-edged shards of York stone flags, gyrating windmill arms for balance, smooth-soled leather brogues slipping on the shallow end steps, catapulting me feet-first into the icy drink, a human torpedo breaking the bubbling surface gasping, finding my feet spluttering, forcibly treacle-wading, twisting through the deepening water panting, desperate panic pushing against dragging drenched clothes; adrenaline-powered breast-stroke legs kicking, arms pulling towards our floating, half-submerged, upside down, swimming goggles-wearing, drowned pet rhino, Mr Richard.

Mixer tap chlorinated water, tears and sweat abseil down my bleached face, as I stretch sopping cuff-linked, shirt-sleeved arms upwards, straining against my sodden jacket, neck deep, jumping upwards, bouncing to push off his stiff legs attached squashy orange swimming bands, jostled by his cold, wet, big chunky bulk, as I try to jiggle-wiggle them up and over his bulging three-toed feet – discount purchased because we had to buy two pairs, which, quite unexpectedly, included a free rainbow-coloured rubber ring, more than likely a loss leader promotion, and inserted with the gratis gift was a printed A5 marketing flyer, offering a tempting 15% discount on future online purchases – properly knackered, blowing, bedraggled in my submerged Carl Stuart tailored pinstripe suit, bespoke Egyptian cotton, double-cuffed, huntsman collared, Mother of Pearl button-up shirt and hand-sewn silk tie, all now ruined, much like my underwater Dan Nelson handmade brogues; immersed, stood sobbing while he bobs, rolling bloated.

I still can't believe he's gone if I'm honest, and the police are continuing their investigation based on the fact that he'd had numerous swimming lessons without his inflatable leg bands, including passing his swimming proficiency award in his trunks and pyjamas with flying colours, which included retrieving a black rubber brick from the bottom of the local leisure centre pool, and therefore he was actually very confident in the water, evidenced by his framed, dining room wall-mounted certificate, but the goldfish don't seem to understand or even care, despite my attempts at breaking the sad news, speaking slowly and pouting, nose squashed up against the condensation-misted side of the glass fish tank. Anyway, we decided to bury Mr Richard upside down at the end of the garden, both out of respect and as a much-needed artistic addition to compliment the barbecue area, making a feature out of his vertical, rigor mortis legs painted red, toenails white, the soles of his feet perfect toadstool seats for guests sat chatting, drinks in hand, others standing and all around the new bespoke fitted decking, which matches the garden shed.

Weirdly, our snake doesn't sleep in the toilet anymore. Instead, he prefers to slither off to the garden and curl up atop one of Mr Richard's toadstool seat feet. The cats often sneak out to join him, taking up the other three places; the dogs run riot, chasing each other up and down the stairs knowing the coast is clear, and then go outside to urinate over Mr Richard's tree stump legs and the snake and the cats as they sleep!

Apparently, the police are now trying to secure a court order to dig up our back garden, as our neighbours from across the road opposite also had a loss in the family recently, when their poultry pet, Rebecca the chicken, was found floating in their paltry garden pond but I'm reliably informed that foul play is not suspected and luckily for us they decided to slow oven roast her in a mouth-watering honey and lemon glaze, stuffed to the gunnels with scrumptious, homemade sage and onion stuffing rather than bury her because we really enjoyed eating her when we were kindly invited over for an ambrosial Sunday lunch, with delectable duck fat-roasted King Edward potatoes and luscious, homegrown, crispy garlic parmesan-roasted carrots, and divine roasted buttered parsnips, heavenly Dale End cheddar cauliflower cheese, peppered swede, butter-braised cabbage, glorious Maris Piper fluffy mash potato, rhino crackling and traditional square tin Yorkshire pudding cooked in traditional beef dripping, with lashings of delicious thick, bubbling, cara-melised onion gravy and freshly picked, homemade, fiery hot, creamy horseradish sauce, complemented by a wonderful chilled Chablis Chardonnay, as both my wife and I have already confirmed in our written police witness statements.

Zebras Crossing

Now you see me, now you don't; I'm a zebra, you see, or maybe you don't? A kind of horse, an African equid, conspicuous with patterned, vertical black and white-coloured stripes, up and down all over me, unless I'm stood on a zebra crossing, whatever that might be.

Some say I look like a giant, misshapen humbug, and apparently I'm just as sweet to eat, although I do not know what a humbug is, but according to the lions and crocodiles of the African continent, I really am a tasty treat! Their modus operandi, though, is not to suck and roll zebras around inside their mouths. No, these beasts prefer to tear zebras apart, a razor-clawed gang of snarling, canine-toothed lions surrounding and tucking into their defeated, prostrate feast, or ancient crocodiles, jaws locked, dragging a zebra to drown in muddy waters asunder; rolling, rolling, rolling and keep on rolling, rolling, rolling to separate raw hide and flesh from bone, their plunder!

Zebras live on the great African plains, or in zoos around the world, so I've heard, or figuratively speaking, in painted black and white marked stripes spread out alternately across roads, as part of Belisha-beaconed zebra crossings, which allow humans to safely walk from one side of the street to the other.

I only know this because, as I stand in the shade of a large baobab tree, I am reading the description of a zebra crossing, in English, from Great Britain's Department for Transport Highway Code booklet, which I found discarded on the savanna at sunset. It is somewhat dirty and wild dog-eared, to be honest, and must have been dropped by a safari tourist.

Anyway, from what I've read, a zebra crossing is not some barmy, solitary, mad as a balloon zebra nutter, 'I'm a teapot!' bonkers fruitcake with a death wish, running hell for leather, jumping *'Yeeha!'* into the Zambezi River, delicious food on the go for submerged beady-eyed crocodiles, peeking above the water line as they wait for their crazed Olympic feat, *in a while, crocodile!* Uber Eats delivery of fresh meat.

Zebra crossings are not zebras crossing, either, which is a bonkers herd of barmy, cross-eyed, tongue-flapping zebra nutters, who for reasons unknown – possibly severe sunstroke – have all decided to take an early bath as they trot on treading water, a veritable vittles conveyor belt of zebra zushi!

Today's special offer for the bask of crocodiles is: *Eat as much as you like!*

Just as it was yesterday, and the day before and the day before that, and the day before that and the day before that, and the day… well, you get the picture. No wonder the lolling crocodiles are all laid out laughing!

All the way to the muddy bank, as they cruelly sneak up and pounce on zebras unannounced, pulling them back, reversing to disappear, when zebras ought to scarper like hell, head down, hooves to the ground, lion-chased on the plain in the clear, leaving them for dust, not trapped flailing in bloody water!

As a joker in the pack said recently: 'It's not an all you can eat buffet, it's an all you can eat buffalo!'

Sorry, I digress (again!).

The description of a zebra crossing starts with a warning, according to Great Britain's Highway Code booklet, and reads as follows:

18
You MUST NOT loiter on any type of crossing.
Laws ZPPPCRGD reg 19 & RTRA sect 25(5)

Now, let's consider this, shall we?

You MUST NOT loiter...

Hmm, how interesting!

Both zebras and humans are obviously given the same warning as, coincidentally, the matriarchs of the zebra community are always repeatedly lecturing the gathered herds of youngsters on Zebra Golden Rule Number One.

<u>Zebra Golden Rule No.1</u>

When crossing the plain or crossing through water, do not stop, do not loiter!

What it doesn't say is that you must not walk slowly, so all those dillydallying, dawdling zebras are actually not committing an offence; all they are doing, in fact, is delaying everyone and making them late, compared to the loitering zebra nutters who completely stop the flow of zebra traffic, so everyone becomes tempting bait at greater risk of being eaten by the crocodiles or lions, who, ironically, lay in wait.

If these bloody idiots survive, they are most definitely fined for loitering and could even find themselves in zebra court, as the infamous 'Zebra Three' found to their surprise and cost.

'What's that?' you ask.

It's not just kangaroos that have courts, you know!

19

Zebra crossings. Give traffic plenty of time to see you and to stop before you start to cross.

Unfortunately, we zebras are stuck between a muddy rock and a tough flat fish based on this zebra crossing rule, because if we were to follow it to the letter, and unfortunately some nutters do, we literally would be sitting ducks – that is to say, loitering zebras – and quite frankly, if crocodiles or lions can't see our black and white striped-patterned bodies, inconspicuous as a ruddy African bush fire in the middle of the night, and therefore perfect camouflage, of course, against the golden-hued savanna, then what's the bloody point of us four-legged humbugs in the first place, because contrary to human road users, who impatiently wait at zebra crossings, lions and crocodiles wait patiently for zebras to cross!

You see, unlike you humans, we zebras don't have doctors and nurses or the NHS, or any sort of health-care systems at all; we don't even get treated for stress! Although, we did have a police force once, and it was good to see the young recruits earning their stripes, but the extortionate Z cars insurance premiums took the lion's share of the budget, and after chewing it over for some time, it was sadly disbanded.

Now we just rely on safety in numbers as we watch one another's backs; using our speed and agility, and our ability to buck and kick out our hind legs, our powerful hooved pistons, when we are under attack.

Sorry, excuse me for a moment!

'Hey, giggle chops! Keep the bloody noise down and leave the giraffe alone, will you? I'm trying to read over here!

'What? I've got some brass neck? I think you mean my elongated friend there!

'Oh, what's wrong, have you lost your babysitter? Well, let me help. So, the cackle crèche is that way – just follow your nose until you reach the edge of the cliff and keep going.

'What, square up?

'You're having a laugh, aren't you?

'Am I going to have to take off my stripy coat?

'Hey, I'm warning you! Back off and leave Walter alone, before I kick your butt so hard, your mum will feel it!

'Really?

'D'you wanna go, bro?

'Do you?

'Are you absolutely sure?

'Really?

'You really wanna go?

'OK then, have you bought a ticket?

'A ticket! Have you bought one?

'Great, then get ready to ride the pain train! All aboard!'

Oh dear, sorry about that! Unforeseen obstreperous hyena interruption. Just needed to put my hoof down!

'My pleasure, Walter, don't mention it. See you on the savanna!'

I beg your pardon!

As I once said to my mate, Pegasus the pelican, puffin' away after I saved the day, 'Toucan play at that game!'

Anyway, from what I've been told, the majority of you humans have never even seen a zebra in the flesh, except in a zoo or on a television, whatever that is, but why a zebra would stand on a television I can only imagine and only ever think of the word *zebra* as you step onto black and white-painted road stripes, nonchalantly lifting your foot off the pavement to touch the tip of your toe to the tarmac, bumper cars bashing, skidding, slamming into one another – *CRASH!* – as you nonchalantly saunter proudly across, slower than a giant African snail!

The centre of your own bloody wallowing universe!

Stationary drivers watching your moment of personified power in the spotlight, shooting daggers at you as you arrogantly drag your feet, glaring at you taking a bloody hour and squeezing every sour, megalomaniac last drop while you drive everyone round the bloody bend!

194
Allow pedestrians plenty of time to cross and do not harass them by revving your engine or edging forward.

'Come on, hurry up!'

'Get a move on!'

'Move your arse!'

'Take your time, why don't you!'

'Could you cross any slower?'

They say to themselves (and much worse!) as they glower! Why don't you just spread out a bloody blanket and lay down and relax, and uncork a bottle of full-bodied Merlot while you're at it, they wonder! Oh, don't worry about us road tax-paying car drivers, we've got all bloody day! In fact, why not have a picnic with bloody Tickler cheese and crackers, or better still, open up that Fortnum & Mason's hamper you bought, you slowcoach, selfish swine, because we've got all the time in the world to take legal action and prosecute, as you are now loitering rather than dawdling, so see you in court! Or so I was entertainingly told by a well-read equine friend, who apparently was told by a returning swallow.

It is also quite amazing what a zebra can pick up by listening to the talkative tourists, hence the reason I'm wearing a black leg band, although you probably wouldn't see it as I stand head-down grazing, posing for photographs. You see, we are all in mourning, and even the crocodiles are welling up because a rhinoceros relative of a friend of mine recently drowned in some sort of swimming pool accident in England, poor old chap, but it has reinforced our determination to teach our youngsters how to swim, with or without inflatable leg bands.

Fly Me to the Moon

'He's flying to the moon, you know. Well, that's what he said anyway.'

'What?'

'Arthur's flying to the moon.'

'Eh, when?'

'Next week, he said.'

'Next week?'

'Yes, that's what he said. He told me this morning as he got out of bed, but you know what, I think he's still recovering from that bump on his head!'

'One minute, sorry. Eh, Arthur, are you flying to the moon?'

'What?'

'I said, are you flying to the moon?'

'Oh, yes! Yes, I am!'

'When?'

'What?'

'When are you going?'

'Oh, erm, a week today!'

'When?'

'Next Saturday lunchtime.'

'He's such an idiot, bless him. His head's a shed!' Jean, Arthur's wife, says to her friend Sandra, as they sit and chat while drinking tea at the kitchen table.

'Just a second, Jean, let me ask him something,' Sandra says, before calling into the living room, 'Hey, Arthur!'

'What is it?' Arthur cries. 'I'm trying to watch the horse racing!'

'How are you going to get to the moon?'

'How d'ya think? In my rocket, of course!'

'What rocket?'

'The bloody rocket that's going to fly me there!'

Arthur sits back in his worn, faded brown, sunken leather armchair in the fuliginous, discoloured white wood chip wallpapered lounge, watching Saturday afternoon horse racing on BBC One's *Grandstand*, creased, hand-rolled lit cigarette stuck overhanging between blue-tinged lips at the side of his mouth, coiling smoke trail rising, curling up into peroxide net curtain-filtered sunlight. The round, silver-coloured tin ashtray, overflowing with white, wizened maggot, discarded cigarette ends sits on the left arm of his chair, where he reclines opposite the rediffusion black-and-white television set, with his tobacco tin and ciga-rette papers resting precariously behind it. A chipped, tea-drained and stained white cup and saucer sit on the opposite arm, all perpendicular to the crackling coal fire, splinter wood spitting behind the old meshed metal fire guard-protected hearth, dully reflected in the large, dimple-dented, Mick Jagger-lipped brass coal scuttle bucket, half full and dormant by the fireplace, with the shovel handle sticking out and the brass pan head resting inside, on top of the coal, and a hearth brush, poker and fireside tongs brass companion set, with one hanging tool absent, standing sentry on the opposite side of the hearth. A letter-strewn, decorative brass mail rack and an assortment of lacklustre brass ornaments clutter the mantelpiece on either side of an antique Victorian walnut mantel clock, placed below a hanging desilvered-edged overmantel mirror.

Sandra smiles quizzically, holding her teacup in both hands and resting her elbows on the table, and looks at her friend with concern. 'Don't you think you should take him to the doctors again, Jean?' she asks.

'No, he's fine,' Jean says, 'he just needs to rest, that's all. He always wants penny and ha'penny, take no notice.'

'Well, he certainly has a vivid imagination.'

'You can say that again!'

'Makes me laugh, though.'

'He makes everybody laugh!'

They both pause to drink their tea, sitting opposite each other at the kitchen table, with the dark blue, hand-knitted, ribbed woollen pom-pom tea cosy-covered teapot on a circular, corn-coloured, beaded teapot mat between them. The grandfather clock in the hallway chimes on the hour, interrupting their thoughts and drowning out the horse racing commentary in the back-ground, and both Sandra and Jean replace their cups in their saucers.

'Arthur?' Sandra says, raising her voice.

'What?'

'Could I ask you something?'

'Wait a minute, I can hardly hear you. You sound like a bloody Dalek! Let me turn the telly down a bit,' Arthur shouts, before half-rising with a groan and leaning over towards the television set. He stretches to turn down the volume by twisting the sound knob on the front panel, and then slumps back down into his seat. 'That's better. Right, what were you saying?'

'Can you ride tandem?'

'What's that?'

'Can you ride tandem?'

'What you on about?'

'Don't you see, you could take your Jean with you to the moon?' Sandra explains, and then, looking at Jean and smiling, she sings,

'But you'll look sweet up on the seat of a bicycle built for two!'

Jean giggles and applauds.

'I'm flying to the moon in a rocket, not on a bloody bicycle, you silly sod!' Arthur replies irritably.

'I don't want to go to the moon anyway,' Jean says, frowning. 'I get bloody car sick just walking to the shops, so you can forget about that for a game of soldiers! Hey love,' she calls into the living room, 'd'you remember that time when that old man was sick on the bus?'

'When?' Arthur asks.

'You know, when we were on the bus on our way home from that day trip to York?'

'Aye, I do! Don't you mean, *The Grand Old Puke of York!*' he sings, chuckling.

'Aye, that's him. Poor old bugger!' Jean laughs. 'D'you remember his missus trying to help, and her getting covered head-to-toe after slipping in it!' She pulls a sour face, as if sucking a lemon, which Sandra mimics.

'And when he puked up, he puked up, and when she slipped and fell in it, she slipped and fell in it, and when she was kneeling halfway up all covered in it, she was neither up nor down!' Arthur sings, laughing his socks off.

'Stop it now, Arthur! Bloody hell, you're going to give me a hernia!' Jean shouts, laughing as Sandra throws her head back, shoulders wobbling and eyes closed, cackling. 'You are a funny bugger, my Arthur, my little chucky egg.' She uses her pinafore to mop her teary eyes.

'Thanks, love,' Arthur replies, having calmed down.

'Oh, bloody hell! OK, rocket man, back to earth,' Sandra says, gasping, while repeatedly wiping her eyes with the back and palm of her hand. 'So, when you get to the moon in your rocket, what are you going to do then?'

'A grand old puke!'

'Come on, Arthur, I'm interested,' Sandra says in all seriousness.

'Oh, I don't know, do I! I'll probably walk around for a bit, like, and then I'll put my flag in the ground and find a rock to sit on, so I can eat my cheese and pickle sandwiches and drink my flask of tea, and then I'll look back at planet earth and wave at everybody.'

'You're kidding, aren't you?'

'No, I'm bloody tellin' you what I'm gonna do!'

'Arthur, stop pulling Sandra's leg, will you,' Jean raises her voice. 'You'll have the neighbours talking!'

'It's a bit too bloody late for that, love!' Arthur chuckles.

'Anyway, which flag?' Sandra enquires.

'What's this, twenty bloody questions? I'm tryin' to watch the nags on the telly!' Arthur says, squeezing his roll-up between tight lips, as Peter O'Sullivan's horse racing commentary cranks up a notch.

'You said you were going to put a flag on the moon,' Sandra reminds him.

'I am. *My* flag!'

'What's your flag, then?'

'Bloody hell!' he erupts, exasperated, putting out his fag by twisting his rust-tipped fingers and crushing it into the side of the ashtray. 'OK, are you listening? It's white like the St George's flag, but instead of a red cross, it will say *ARTHUR WAS HERE!*'

'Bloody hell, that's brilliant.'

'Yeah, I thought so, too!'

'What if you held the flag up high and waved it around? Maybe Jean and I could see you on the moon through your binoculars.'

'I'm taking my binoculars with me.'

'Oh, well, I could borrow a pair from someone, couldn't I, Jean?'

'Will you give it a rest, the pair of you, for goodness' sake?' Jean sighs and shakes her head, before lowering her voice and whispering, 'You shouldn't encourage him, Sandra!'

'Well, it's just something to talk about, isn't it?' Sandra says quietly.

'Say that again!' Jean exhales, securing her teacup in its saucer and pushing her chair back, she rises to check on the food she is cooking.

Putting on her beige oven gloves that are hanging next to the stove, she opens the oven door to check on her homemade steak and kidney pie, steam escaping as she instinctively winces at the invisible wall of heat instantly hitting her face and, satisfied with the almost fully risen, golden brown-topped pastry crust, she quickly closes the oven door and takes off her oven gloves and, picking up the wooden spoon laid next to the stove, she lifts off the three saucepan lids containing water-boiling new potatoes, swede and cabbage. Placing them aside, she gently stirs the vegetables in each pan, and turns and opens a draw and takes out a pointed knife, before turning back to the stove and hovering over the bubbling potatoes, holding the wooden spoon handle with her right hand as she scoops up a single boiled potato (a steaming race horse being led into the winners enclosure) and drains off the hot water by turning the handle to press and hold the potato against the inside of the saucepan. Then, turning the wooden spoon upwards and cradling it in the concaved oval head, she prods the potato, piercing it with the tip of the knife in her left hand to test if it is cooked. Gently replacing it back into the bubbling water, she repeats the 'steaming racehorse' action by scooping up a chunk of swede and a wedge of cabbage respectively, before putting both utensils back onto the yellow Formica worktop. Bending over, she then checks all three electric rings, twisting each knob to the low heat setting before replacing the saucepan lids slightly off-kilter to allow the heat to escape while the vegetables simmer, and carefully lifts the enamel kettle up off the back of the stove, shaking it to gauge the water content and sidestepping to the sink, where she fills it at the cold tap by flipping open the spout cap. She then gently replaces the full kettle down on the stove, and turns on the electric coil ring to the low heat setting with a twist of the knob. Wiping her hands on her pink pinafore, she walks back to the kitchen table to retake her seat opposite her friend.

Pulling her chair in, she pours herself and Sandra a top-up from the cosied teapot, firstly adding milk to both cups from the small, white jug sat close at hand, next to the decorative oriental tea caddy on the faded yellow, flower-patterned, plastic tablecloth, and then picking up the silver tea strainer off its stand she places it over each cup and pours the piping hot tea individually into both cups.

'Hey, Arthur!' Sandra calls out again, elbows resting on the table and teacup held in both hands, as she blows down onto the hot tea with pursed lips, rippling the surface.

'What now?' Arthur asks.

'Is it true that you and Jean always drink the leftover hot water after cooking your vegetables?'

'Aye, we do, don't we, love.'

'Always!' Jean confirms. 'Full of natural goodness.'

'I've often wondered where Jean got her lovely complexion from,' Sandra says, head cocked, looking at her friend with a smile, as Jean tuts and shakes her head, somewhat embarrassed.

'Oh, and what about *my* lovely complexion?' Arthur asks sarcastically.

'You're a bloody bloke, so you don't have a complexion!' Jean laughs.

'Charming!'

'Do you want to try some?' Jean asks her friend. 'The vegetables are nearly ready, so I can pour you some, if you like?'

'Oh no, not for me, thanks, Jean. Tea's my only tipple and nowt else, you know that!'

'Well, there's always plenty of that to go around, that's for sure, but don't ever be afraid to ask.'

'Hey, Arthur, did Jean ever tell you?' Sandra asks excitedly.

'Tell me what?'

'Tell him what?' Jean asks.

'I was thinking of opening a pub on the moon, you know,' Sandra says.

'Really?' Jean asks, puzzled.

'Yeah, but I decided not to bother, because it wouldn't have any atmosphere!' Sandra smirks.

'Oh, Sandra!' Jean exclaims, laughing and dribbling drops of tea onto the table. She quickly puts her cup down onto the saucer, coughing as she lifts up her pinafore to wipe her mouth, and then uses it to dab the miniature tabletop puddles.

'You daft bugger!' Arthur shouts from the lounge.

'Anyway, when are we actually going to see this rocket of yours then, Arthur?' Sandra enquires.

'Not more bloody questions!' he groans.

'Come on, Arthur, when are we going to see it?' she presses him.

'Now that would be telling, wouldn't it?'

'Oh, come on, don't be a spoilsport!'

'You'll see it in good time.'

'But I want to see it now!'

'Well, you can't, so hold your bloody horses!'

'But I want to!'

'Well, you bloody can't, so stop askin'!'

'Oh, Arthur, but I'm so excited!'

'You'll just have to wait like everybody else, won't ya!'

'I don't think I can.'

'It's only a bloody week, so calm down!'

'OK, Arthur, I'll wait, but can I be the first to see it?'

'Of course, love, no problem.'

'Fantastic! Did you hear that, Jean? He's going to let me be the first to see it!'

'Well, bully for you,' Jean takes a sip of tea while staring at her friend in disbelief.

'You don't seem too happy about it.'

'Sandra, he doesn't have a rocket, it's all in his head!'" Jean says, lowering her voice.

'Are you sure?'

'I'm absolutely bloody positive!'

'But what if he does have one?'

'He doesn't!'

'You don't know that.'

'I bloody do!'

'No, you don't!'

'OK, look, if he's got a rocket to fly him to the moon, where the hell is it, under the bed? Oh no, I forgot, it's in the bloody garden shed,' Jean tuts and rolls her eyes.

'Well, you've got a bloody big garden shed!'

'It's not Dr Who's bloody Tardis, Sandra!'

'I don't know, do I, but he must have one, otherwise how is he going to get there? On the number forty-eight bus?'

'No, he's going to catch the train.'

'Don't be daft, they're too bloody heavy!'

'Oh, you're as barmy as he is!' Jean laughs.

'Well, I can't believe his own wife, my best friend, doesn't believe her own husband!'

'I think it's you who needs to see the bloody doctor, not him!'

'No, I bloody don't! Hey, Arthur, your Jean here doesn't believe you've got a rocket to fly you to the moon!' Sandra bellows.

'Tell me about it!' Arthur answers.

'It's called trust, Jean!' Sandra smirks at her friend.

'No, Sandra, it's called being as nutty as a bloody fruitcake!'

'Honestly!' Sandra exclaims, frowning.

'Tittle-tattle tell-tale!' Jean sticks out her tongue.

'Pack it in for a minute, you two, and listen,' Arthur interjects from his armchair, 'I've got something to tell my dear wife. Now then, Jean, when I take off in my rocket and land on the moon, the first thing I'm going to do is to draw a big heart in the moon dust and write our names in it. What about that, then, eh?'

'Ah, you big softy!' Jean's face instantly brightens. 'I do love you!'

'Oh, how romantic, Jean!' Sandra says, placing a hand on her friend's arm as her eyes start to well up.

'And if you believe that, you'll believe bloody anything!' he adds, laughing until he's coughing. He leans over and pulls a crumpled, off-white handkerchief from his right trouser pocket, into which he loudly blows his spider angiomas, purple-tipped nose.

Meanwhile, Jean, obviously upset and averting her friend's shocked gaze, takes out her own tissue from her pinafore pocket and dabs her eyes with a resigned smile, as the kettle on the stove starts whistling manically and rising, she leaves the table to put on her oven gloves once again.

'And another thing, where's my bloody lunch?' Arthur yells. 'My stomach thinks my throat's been cut!'

Day of Launch (Saturday Lunchtime).

'Arthur! Arthur!' Jean shouts up from the bottom of the stairs.

'I'm on the bog!' Arthur replies.

'You're going to be late!'

'What?'

'You're going to be late for your trip to the moon!'

'Alright, calm down! I've just got to put on my space suit and helmet, and then I'll be ready.'

'Everyone's outside waiting, Arthur. The neighbours, the local bobby, the town's brass band, the mayor, the local paper and a photographer – everyone! Even Chalbert's fish and chip van is here!'

'Bloody hell, no pressure then!' he mutters to himself. 'Alright, I'm coming, don't get your knickerbockers in a twist!'

'I'll put the kettle on and make you a cuppa, alright?'

'Thanks, love!' he shouts, flushing the toilet and walking across the creaking landing into the bathroom to wash his hands.

Word has spread about Arthur's trip to the moon, and now crowds of tea-drinking, fish and chips-eating locals have gathered in the street outside his house in anticipation. Neighbours, in slippers and coats, some wearing headscarves and rollers, surrounded by scampering children, and uniformed brass band musicians stand in groups chatting, mugs and crinkled old newspapers steaming in their hands, while the mayor joins the orderly, salivating queue on the pavement for a Chalbert's pattie and chips lunch. The local bobby has also turned up to keep an eye on proceedings, and is standing at the front door.

'Arthur, your tea's getting cold!' Jean shouts up from the bottom of the stairs again.

'OK, I'll be down in a minute!'

'Oh, Arthur! Arthur!'

'Hell's bells, what is it now?'

'Arthur, there's a reporter from the *News of the World* at the back door, saying he wants an interview!'

'Tell him to bugger off! The local rag already promised me a full-page spread.'

'He won't listen! He says he'll pay us money if you give him an interview.'

'He said he's going to pay us?'

'That's what he said.'

'Ask him how much.'

'He said he would pay us five pounds cash.'

'Five pounds cash?'

'That's what he said.'

'Let me get my gear on and I'll be down.'

'OK, but hurry up. Your tea's getting cold and I need to go to the post office to get some stamps. It's Sandra's birthday next week and I need to send her a card.'

'Nothin' like getting your bloody priorities right!' he shouts from the bedroom.

'What do you mean?' she replies, stood hands on hips at the bottom of the stairs.

'I'm flying to the moon, and you're worried about getting a bloody birthday card for Sandra!'

'She's my best friend!'

'And I'm your bloody astronaut husband!'

'Oh, Arthur, stop being so childish and hurry up. Your tea's getting cold!'

Arthur exhales, glancing at the ceiling as he pulls his flannel grey spacesuit suit trousers up over his frayed long johns, zipping them up as he buttons his granddad shirt over his vest and pulls on his white polo neck jumper, and then tucks all the layers into his trousers before finally buttoning them at the waist and fixing his striped clip-on braces, alternately stretching them upwards and hooking them individually with each thumb to secure them over his shoulders. Bending down, he folds in the trouser material from his shins to his ankles and pulls his old black-and-white-hooped rugby socks up and over them, fastening both legs with bicycle clips above the ankles before rising to grab his elbow- and knee-patched model railway enthusiast orange overalls off the bed, and shaking them open width-ways at the hips, he slips his legs in, pulling them up around and past his waist, pushing each arm in and out at the sleeves and pulls the shoulders and collar up and over his upper body and turning down the collar, he finally zips up the front and stands looking at himself in the antique Cheval mahogany mirror in the corner of the bedroom. Pleased with his reflection and flattening down his receding, pomaded hair (unaware that he perfectly resembles the *'Before application'* photo in a weekly-ran national newspaper classified ad for a hair rejuvenation product), he sits down on the edge of the pink towelling bedspread, next to his motorcycle gloves, open-faced moped motorcycle helmet, goggles and a second pair of bicycle clips, and lifts up and bends his right leg to fold in the overall material at the ankle, attaching the third bicycle clip and then gripping the rubber-top edge at either side with each hand, he pushes his foot down into one of his brand-new, steel toe-capped wellington moon boots.

Jean, meanwhile, is at the kitchen door handing the *News of the World* reporter a cup of tea. 'There you go, love, but keep it quiet,' she says. 'There's a crowd out front, and I don't want to start a stampede.'

'Or a cafe!' the reporter quips.

'Oh no, thank you very much! It's enough cooking for my Arthur, let alone the bloody neighbours!'

'Oh yeah, I can imagine. Well, thanks for the drink, missus,' the reporter nods, shouldering his camera as he steps forward and takes hold of the teacup and saucer, complete with two circular biscuits, in both hands. 'Oh, and thanks for the chocolate digestives, too!'

'No trouble, love,' Jean says smiling .

'Is Arthur nearly ready then, Mrs Benn?'

'Aye 'appen, I think so. He's just putting on his helmet and he'll be down.'

'Good, I'll wait here then, and thanks again for the tea.'

'Don't mention it, love. Let me go indoors and make sure he's gettin' a move on, alright?'

She closes the back door as the reporter leans his rain mac-encased shoulder against the terraced house's rear brickwork, facing the narrow lawn in their sunny back garden, divided by a crazy paving stoned path down the middle, with hydrangea and chrysanthemum borders running parallel along the edges, and a wooden-propped looping clothesline with plain-coloured, billowing bed sheets pegged out, attached to vertical poles at either side, all in front of a drab concrete coal shed at the rear, itself opposite the garden shed. Teacup and saucer in hand, he sips his breeze-wrinkled steaming tea.

Jean, on the other hand, has picked up Arthur's lukewarm cup of tea, which she carries through to the bottom of the hallway stairs.

'Arthur, are you- oh!' she begins to shout up again, but freezes mid-sentence at the sight of him walking down the stairs in full astronaut attire, seemingly in slow motion, carrying his home made flag. Jean stares open-mouthed as the teacup and saucer falls from her grip to hit the floor, spilling tea across the bottom of the stairs and the hallway rug.

'Fly me to the moon, and let me play among the stars!' Arthur sings, as a policeman's distorted face briefly appears in the wavy, rippled glass oval front door window.

Jean stands gobsmacked as black wellington boot-wearing, orange overall over white polo neck-clad, open-faced motorcycle moped helmet and goggles and gloves-attired Arthur the astronaut arrives at the bottom of the stairs.

'Any chance of another cuppa, love?' he asks, smiling as he hands her his flag. 'I just need to get me scarf and coat and then I'm off.' He strides past his wife towards the coat stand in the corner of the hallway near the front door, motorcycle goggles already misting up, and steps on the teacup that Jean dropped, crushing it. 'One small step for man, one giant problem for womankind!'

He frowns, looking down inquisitively through misted goggles, having felt the teacup underneath his boot for a split second before accidentally breaking it into a dozen pieces underfoot, the sound of which has awoken Jean from her trance, as she joins him in looking down at the pieces of china crockery scattered across the hallway.

'Oh, Arthur, for goodness' sake, take off your bloody goggles will you, before you trip and break your neck!' Jean says. 'They're misted up right good and proper!'

'Alright, don't cry over spilt tea!' Arthur shakes his head, as he slides his scarf off the coat stand.

'Oh, Arthur, honestly, it's all over the hallway! Thank goodness I'm wearing my slippers. You're such a clumsy clot!'

'Well, you dropped the bloody thing.'

'Only after you scared me half to death!'

'Nobody's perfect, are they, but I'm as close as you'll get!' he laughs.

'Talk about blowing your own trumpet!' she frowns, surveying the mess. 'You'll be playing in the brass band next.'

'Alright, alright, at least I didn't crack Jenny's teacup.'

'What?'

'Never mind! Just rushing to get ready, that's all. I've got a tight bloody schedule to keep, don't forget.'

'What? You sound like an American working at NASA or something!' she puts down his flag on the bottom stair, and then bends to soak up spilled tea with the tissue kept inside her pinafore pocket.

'How do you think I'm flying to the moon?'

'Give over, Arthur, honestly! You and your imagination,' she crouches down and picks up the saucer, handing it to her husband. 'Be a love and put that in the kitchen for me, would you? I can't believe it didn't break, the way it went flying. Just shows, you get what you pay for!'

She starts to delicately pick up fragments of teacup, placing them inside her outstretched pinafore which is covering her knees, as Arthur steps past her towards the kitchen, saucer in hand, having finally pulled up his motorcycle goggles.

'I'll just have a quick word with the News of the World reporter out back,' he says, 'and then I'm off.'

'Alright, love,' Jean replies over her shoulder. 'I'll make you another quick cuppa then, shall I? Then you can be on your way.'

'No need, love, I won't have time to drink it!'

'You're not landing on the bloody moon without something hot inside you! It'll only take a minute.'

'Alright, love, but make it quick. I've got a rocket to catch, or should I say, a flying saucer!' he grins, holding up the chipped-edged piece of crockery as he heads towards the kitchen.

'Silly bugger!' Jean mutters, rising up, sagging pinafore held outstretched in both hands, as she ambles into the kitchen and carefully empties the shards of bone china, gently shaking them out of her pinafore into the bin with the tea-soaked tissue, while Arthur can be heard discussing how clement the weather is for the time of year with the newspaper reporter in the back garden.

'Here you go, love, a lovely hot cuppa to warm you up,' she says, handing Arthur a saucer cradling a fresh cup of tea.

'Eh, by gum! Thanks, love, and what about a top-up for our friend here?' he gestures towards the reporter.

'No more for me, thanks. Here you go, love,' the reporter says, handing his empty teacup and saucer back to Jean. 'That was grand.'

'Are you sure?' Jean asks. 'I've also got a lovely Battenberg that needs eating up.'

'Thanks a lot, missus, but the digestives filled a hole, so I'm fine. I just want to finish interviewing Arthur, get some photos and then I'll skedaddle!'

'Oh, alright then. What about you, Arthur?'

'No, I'm fine, love, but you could put a couple of slices of Battenberg in my pack-up, and then I can have cake with my flask of tea on the moon.'

'Great idea!' she beams. 'I'll do that now then, love, and I'll fill your flask with hot tea and put your pack-up sandwich box with your flask in your satchel by the front door. Don't be long now – time is getting on! Oh, and before I forget, I found your bobble hat. It was on your station master chair in the loft, next to your model railway, so I'll put that with your flag by the front door, alright? Oh, and I found your binoculars in the downstairs cupboard, so I'll put them by the front door as well.'

'Alright, thanks very much, love.'

'Now, you're sure that you haven't forgotten anything, Arthur?'

'Wait a minute!' he says, holding his teacup and saucer in his left hand, and moving his right hand up and down, right and left. 'Spectacles, testicles, wallet and watch!'

The reporter bursts out laughing.

'Oh, honestly!' Jean smiles. 'Well, don't forget that you've left your coat and scarf on the kitchen table.'

'Alright, love, thanks! I'll put them on when I come back inside to collect the rest of my gear, and then make my big appearance at the front door. I won't be long.'

'OK, love,' Jean says, closing the back door and leaving Arthur with the reporter.

Ten Minutes Later...

'Right, Arthur, just one final question, and then we'll go around the front and get some photographs, OK?' the reporter says.

'Champion!' Arthur answers.

'So, where is the proper rocket, then?'

'The proper rocket?'

'Yes, the proper moon rocket. The actual rocket that is going to fly you to the moon. It can't be the one stood in your front garden.'

'Nay, nay, Mr Wilkes!' Arthur says with a heavy West Yorkshire accent .

'Sorry, what?'

'Don't be daft, of course it's not!'

'Oh, I was going to say. So, where is it then?'

'Where's what?'

'The proper rocket that will fly you to the moon?'

'Well, that seems to be the question on everyone's lips!'

'I'm not surprised.'

'Look, I've told nobody owt, but it's all sort of got a bit out of bloody hand!'

'How d'you mean?'

'Well, don't tell her indoors, but you see, there isn't actually a proper rocket, like, you know, like a massive

NASA rocket on a proper launchpad at Cape Canaveral, so to speak. It's more like an Airfix, homemade, life-size model at Cape Ena's Terrace, Subway Street.'

'So, it's not exactly a Thunderbird, but more like a Thora Hird!'

'Aye, somethin' like that, but you must promise not to breathe a word of this, and I'll explain everything, like. No messing around now, though, you must promise not to tell a soul!'

'Scout's honour,' the reporter gives the three-fingered salute.

'Alright then,' Arthur sighs, 'you see, some mates of mine made me a bet.'

'What do you mean, "made you a bet?" What sort of bet?'

'That I couldn't convince everyone that I'm flying to the moon.'

'So, what you're saying then, is that you are not really flying to the moon because there isn't a proper rocket?'

'Oh no, there's a proper rocket alright. I'm just not sure it will get me to the moon!'

'Well, where is it?'

'It's on its way here, on the back of my mate's lorry.'

'So, just to recap, the five-foot-tall rocket I photographed earlier, that's stood in your front garden, that's not the proper rocket you will be flying to the moon in, is it?'

'No, course not! I wouldn't bloody fit in it, would I? I'd have to sit on it like a bloody racehorse, like Slim Pickens in Dr Strangelove! Like I've just told you, that's just like a replica, a model, you know, to promote my adventure, like.'

'And the proper rocket that is going to fly you to the moon is the same?'

'Oh no, it's much bigger, over six-foot, but it's made of the same stuff.'

'What, cardboard and tin foil?'

'No, well, sort of, but reinforced double layers of cardboard, you know, to add strength and flexibility, like, with an inner core of four-by-two wooden battens.'

'Oh, that's a relief! For a moment there, I thought you didn't have a bloody clue what you were doing.'

'Who, me? Arthur the astronaut!'

The reporter laughs politely. 'So, let me get this right. You are flying to the moon in a six-foot-tall cardboard-'

'*Reinforced* cardboard,' Arthur interjects.

'Sorry, reinforced cardboard and wooden-battened, tinfoil-covered rocket, wearing a moped helmet, goggles and gloves, your model railway orange overalls, a coat, scarf and rubber wellies?'

'Steel toe-capped rubber wellies, to be exact.'

'Oh right, steel toe-capped rubber wellies, sorry!'

'Plus, an emergency bobble hat, in case it gets cold.'

'Let's not forget the bobble hat!' the reporter says, adding it to his notepad in capital letters. 'But hang on, how is the rocket powered? I mean, how is it going to take off?'

'Coal!'

'Coal?' the reporter looks bewildered.

'Aye, my mate's a coal merchant, you see. It's his flatbed lorry that's on its way here with my rocket on the back, like, but he's also a bit of a whizz-kid when it comes to steam engines, so he's made a coal and turpentine-driven, steam engine-powered rocket.'

'Turpentine?'

'Oh yes, all the coal has been soaking in an old bath full of it in my mate's garage for well over a month now! It's to help with combustion, ya see, and it's all been packed into the base of the rocket, like, right underneath where I'm going to be stood!'

'*What?*' the reporter splutters, as he continues adding to his notes. 'And you are going to stand on top of all of that in your rubber wellies? I mean, how are you-'

'Reinforced cardboard floor!' Arthur interjects again, grinning.

'Arthur, you must be bloody bar-'

'Covered in a triple layer of tinfoil!'

'Well, Dick Turpentine, with that sort of horsepower underneath you, what could possibly go wrong? But, spontaneous human combustion aside, don't you think you will be turned into a piece of toast on re-entry to the earth's atmosphere, on your return back to earth, after landing on the moon?'

'Well, yes, that is a bit of a worry!'

'Sorry, did I say *toast*? I meant to say, *burned to bloody charcoaled crisp!*'

'Yes, you're right. I hadn't really thought of that.'

'Sorry to put a dampener on proceedings.'

'No, but wait a minute, we did put three layers of tin foil over the cardboard and wooden battens.'

'Oh, why didn't you say so? Everything will be absolutely hunky dory, then. Happy days!'

'Exactly!' Arthur finger-taps his temple with a wink.

'But what if you don't even reach the clouds after take-off? You'll just fall back down to earth like a tin can, won't you?'

'Ah well, yes, but I've got that covered, you see, because we've put a homemade parachute in the nose cone, just in case.'

'Oh, a *homemade* parachute?'

'Yes, my wife and her friend Sandra knitted it. Took them the good part of a year.'

'A knitted parachute?'

'Yes, my wife loves knitting!'

'Knitted from what?'

'Wool, of course. What else?'

'Did you say *wool?*'

'Wool, yes! Anyway, she doesn't know it's for my moon trip. They thought that they were doing it for charity! I had to sneak it out under the cover of darkness, so that neither of them found out.'

'A knitted, woollen parachute stuffed in the nose cone?'

'Aye, it's down there for dancing, lad!' Arthur glances at the reporter's feet, smiling.

'You really have thought of everything, haven't you, Arthur?'

'Well, I'm not called King Arthur for nothin'!'

KING ARTHUR the reporter scribbles in capital letters at the top of his notepad, and then asks, 'So, how do you win the bet, then?'

'Well, that's the whole bloody point! You think I'm bothered about burning up on re-entry or falling from a great height? I'll tell you something for nowt, if I don't win this bet by getting my trip to the moon in the paper, I'm buggered, and then I really will be toast. Burnt, buttered, tarred and feathered!'

'Oh, crumbs! But I thought the local paper were covering it?'

'No, they're paying me nowt, so they can sod off!'

'Oh, so that means you're giving the News of the World an exclusive?'

'For five pounds cash? Of course I bloody am!'

'Great! So, Arthur, where did this bet take place, then?' the reporter asks, chewed-end biro at the ready.

'You're not going to believe this, but it was at the Half Moon pub around the corner!'

'Oh, bloody perfect!' the reporter grins. 'And you only win the bet if your trip to the moon appears in the paper?'

'Oh yes!'

'Oh dear!'

'Look, keep this under your hat, but if I don't get a splash in your Sunday rag, me and the missus will have to do a midnight flit and get the hell out of Dodge!'

'What? *No!*'

'Bloody yes! Haven't you seen the crowds out front? If I don't fly to the bloody moon, there will be a bloody riot.'

'Come on!'

'I'm tellin' ya, I'll be bloody lynched – probably outside the Half Moon pub!'

'Now that's a frontpage headline if ever I heard of one.'

'Give over, lad, don't be bloody daft!'

Suddenly, the back door is flung open as Jean and headscarf-wearing Sandra appear, both breathless, with the 'oom-pah' sound of a brass band and spontaneous clapping and cheering emanating from the crowd at the front of the house.

'Arthur, a lorry has just pulled up on road out front with a rocket on it! Everyone is going bloody mad! Can't you hear them?' Jean cries, ready to burst.

'It's your rocket, Arthur! I can't believe that it's your bloody rocket!' Sandra gasps, beside herself with excitement.

'That's not just my rocket, ladies,' Arthur says. 'It's my rocket to the moon!'

'Oh, Arthur, I'm so proud of you, and I love you so much!' Jean says, stepping off the back doorstep to bear hug her husband, who outstretches his arm to keep his teacup and saucer out of harm's way, as Sandra starts sobbing.

'I love you too, love,' he says, as he attempts to disentangle himself from his wife's embrace, 'but I've got a rocket to catch, so onwards and upwards, and let's get this bloody show on the road shall we, ladies!' He hands his teacup and saucer to his dewy-eyed wife, and gesticulates for both Jean and mascara-streaked-cheeks Sandra to go back indoors.

'So, I'll be seeing you and your camera out front, young man,' he says to the reporter as he steps through the back door, following his wife and Sandra into the kitchen. 'And don't forget, you owe me a fiver!'

One week later...

NEWS OF THE WORLD: **KING ARTHUR THE ASTRONAUT'S MOON BET ROCKETS HIM BLAZING OVER THE GLEN TO HIS LOCAL PUB TO MEET HIS BAND OF DRUNKEN BETTING MEN!**

HALF-COCKED, HOMEMADE MOON ROCKET-FLYING HUMAN FIREBALL, KING ARTHUR THE ASTRONAUT, DOWNS HIS SORROWS BY IGNITING HALF MOON PUB'S THATCHED ROOF AND BURNING DOWN THE HOUSE!

Arthur the astronaut's valiant attempt at winning a bet that he could fly to the moon, made with his mates at his local pub, ended in severe pain and disappoint-ment last Saturday lunchtime, as his homemade card-board and tinfoil rocket failed to take off from his mate's flatbed coal lorry, only to fall over and catch fire, scattering the crowd of onlookers and the town's mayor and brass band to a safe distance (with the assistance of the local bobby), as it ignited the lorry's diesel fuel tank, causing a massive explosion heard across the town, shattering windows within a square mile area and devastating two rows of terraced houses, while ironically catapulting the flaming, Irish-jig-dancing, pants-on-fire Arthur the astronaut, 'Fly Me to the Moon' human fireball, screaming across a quarter of a mile of local airspace into the Half Moon pub's thatched roof, burning the pub to the ground!

As dislocated back, crooked neck, broken wrist, fractured ribs, torn meniscus, sprained ankle, bloodshot eyed, swollen nosed, ruptured eardrum, chipped tooth, burnt buttocks, stubbed toe, singed haired, dented pride, cut and bruised Arthur the astronaut said from his hospital bed, surrounded by his family and friends, 'Although I didn't win the bet to fly to the moon, I did reach for the stars, and that's a bet we can all win if we try!'

Police have since confirmed that they have concluded their investigation into the matter, and that no charges are to be brought against Arthur the astronaut or the

four men initially arrested in connection with the inci-
dent and accused of conspiracy to commit *one small
bet for a man, one giant fireball flight for town kind!*

Light and Dark

Sat in my car watching windscreen rainwater rivulets racing downhill, joining forces to win, instantly halted by splattering kin ending their torrential freefall in fluorescent explosions across the glass, wipers intermittently swipe right-left, fanlike unfolding the drenched high street into view, drearily compressed, a smudged mass of dappled umbrellas jostling for room and position, like aggrieved strangers shoehorned together on a church pew, all elbows and words turning the air blue.

And then a lone blind man appears, conspicuous in a stylish Panama hat dripping and glistening neon rain mac, tap-tap-tap-tapping along behind his white elongated cane, people bottlenecked and tripping, slipping around him like he's a human chicane, seemingly pointing to predict where kamikaze rain will bounce off the pavement again and again and again; as Al Pacino comes to mind, dancing the tango sightless but seeing all, surrounded by light but kept in the dark, sitting in my parked car smoking a Cuban cigar, detruded storm clouds' exuded tears tap dancing noisily on the roof above my head, my window open slightly to expel the smoke, driving rain gate-crashing through the gap instead, and I wonder about what we are and the world we inhabit.

A world I have made with my wife in children we brought to life and cherish beyond words, our proof, as we work to deliver their needs in relentless deeds unsung, mating birds repeatedly feeding their gaping-mouthed chicks with worms or a rabbit suckling it's young, as crushing pressure shouldered is carried along and bolstered by a united fight to defeat the dark with love, truth and hard work, our weapons always unholstered.

Life happens and we have to accept it, whether good or bad there is no exit, for people exist as their world revolves in personal songs they sing to deliver their needs, their wants, their dreams of a life fulfilled, or not, by small steps every day, very often forgot, to pay

their bills and fill their tills and have enough left over
to play, their plot.

The Tree

I stand on swirling, tousled sward buffeted, flapping trousers inflated like an advertising air puppet, coat thrashing, collar pulled up around my neck, rigidly entrenched against blustery wind tunnel weather, squinting eyes streaming, watching a tree gesticulate stretching limbs towards me, reaching out in creaking silence for what reason? To reveal some past treason, which anchored it mute to the spot, unable to evade a staggering sot or castigate a clumsy climbing clot?

A substantial barking dog approaches, all fur in a flurry rippling, ears whirling and stops, lowering its protuberant head to sniff the base of the trunk, tiptoeing around turgescent roots huffing, and raising its leg, leaves a glistening mark in crevices of the rhytidome.

Obstinate Longevous Decrepit

(Adult)

Young nurses and doctors dressed like they've just got out of bed and bloody Sunday school, carrying notes from their mums just in case they need to be excused or to provide proof of being underage, concealing them in the hope of keeping shtum!

Passing by me like I'm not here, a sheet and blanket-covered body or even just a head! A wizened, grey candy floss comb-over-topped bowling ball, sat on a coronation crown cushion, white not red.

Flippin' heck, won't you stop and talk to me instead? Ask me a question, like where are you from or what did you do in your life, because guess what? I'm not quite dead!

Crikey, I must be some sort of superhero, just check my chart, why don't you? Go on, look! Read my name! I'm Mr Invisible, so you can't even see what's wrong with me, eh?

'Nurse, I said remove his spectacles!'

Christ, I'm now laughing at my own jokes, talking to myself like when I was at school with holes in my pockets and I lost my marbles, cursing under my breath, two-bob bit the dust and down the drain and no more pocket money for a week, knowing that my dad was going to go off like a bleedin' rocket!

What's the bloody point?

I may as well be at home, smoking a cigar, single malt in hand, listening to birdsong and the cricket sat in my garden shed.

As my wife once said:

'I'm not here for a long time, I'm here for a good time!'

A nurse! A nurse!

My kingdom for a nurse!

Oh bugger, I spoke too soon!

You wait all day for one, and then four blithering idiots turn up at once! Look at 'em! Who the bloody hell do they think they are? Stood over me now, knebbing, havin' a right good skeg, curtain drawn around so they can get away with bleedin' murder! Familiar faeces of Dr Pinocchio and his crew of nosy bloody parker mates, staring at me like I'm a bloody circus freak or an endangered species in a bleedin' zoo! Dipping their beaks and their bloody thermometers, slapping their cold silver medallions on my chest, nearly giving me a bloody heart attack, rubber-gloved hands to leave no finger prints, checking out my meat and two veg, prodding me like I'm a bloody sponge cake just out of the oven!

'Cor blimey!'

'All the king's horses and all the king's men, eh?'

'Pith off!'

'But, sir, I've only just arrived!'

'Laugh? I nearly bought a round!'

'Give over!'

'Seen enough 'ave ya, or d'ya want a photograph?'

'Take a wild bloody guess!'

'What was that, Dr Twat?'

'My arse, your face?'

'Gerroff!'

'Are you talking to me or chewing a brick?'

'What? You used to be shit hot, but now you're just shit!'

'You couldn't even run a bath!'

'Give over, I said, cloth ears!'

'Get off your high horse!'

'Where are you lot from, then, TWATS R US?'

'Whatever, whatever, Dr Clever.'

'Yeah, you and whose army?'

'Sod off!'

'Sling your bloody hook, will ya!'

'Give it a rest, for Christ's sake!'

'Gerroff, I said!'

'Pack it in!'

'Have you still got your bag for life? Sorry, your wife!'

'Do us all a favour and take a long walk off a short pier!'

'I'd rather stick needles in *your* eyes!'

'Why don't you take a ball apiece and go an' play on the fast lane of the M1?'

'Don't worry, I'll send a plumber around to fix *your* ballcock!'

'Fuck you and the horse you rode in on!'

'You couldn't organise a mayor-saying contest in a field of sheep!'

'On ya bloody bike!'

'Cheerio chin-chin...

... goodbye-ee! See you next Tuesday!'

Telling me this and telling me that, car rear window dog heads nodding at one another, and who gives a shit and blah, blah, blah, blah, blah, bleedin' blah, blah *black sheep, have you any wool?* Around my bed, chin-wagging like a bloody purple rinse sewing circle, dressed in grubby white coats like they work in a bleedin' chicken factory, school kids who know the square route of fuck all! All mouth and no trousers, talkin' the talk, young, dumb and nappies full, crawling the walk, like a broken toilet: full of shit!

'Yes, sir... yes, sir... three bags full, sir!'

Well, I'll tell you what, why don't you try using a bloody iron and a bloody razor and a comb, you creased-shirted, collar undone, stubble chinned, mop-haired, scruffy bastards! Oh, and take your hands out of your pockets, polish your shoes, stand up straight, tuck your bloody shirt in, do your top button up and wear a bloody tie! And you over there, Mr Formula One ice cream van driver, stood dillydallying next to an empty wheelchair, givin' it loads, chattin' up a nurse with your poncey accent and your poncey ponytail, drinking your poncey coffee and now yawning with ya big, fat Mersey Tunnel gob wide open! Cover your cake hole, you rude prick; nobody wants to see the Farley's Rusks that your mum spoon-fed you for breakfast!

What?

Oh, are you feeling tiredy-wiredy?

Diddums!

Do you want me to get your fluffy slippers and dressing gown, and run you a nice hot bubble bath, and make you a lovely hot cup of cocoa and tuck you up in bed? Do you? Well, fuck off and die, you poncey, port out, starboard home, paralysed piece of piss!

Jesus H Christ, bring back national service, for God's sake, and forget the poxy slipper or the bleedin' belt; no, give 'em a right good caning, and tan their arses within an inch of their lives with the bloody birch! That'll shit 'em up and get these mollycoddled good-for-nothings standing to attention, dancing on the spot and howling, doing Knees Up Mother Brown, rubbing their raw backsides and crying out for 'MAMA!'

Oh yes, and a good clip around the lughole for good measure, for cheeking their elders, and a kick in the clems and a bloody good clout to knock 'em into next week, and a right good kick in the shins, and bray 'em if they start with the screaming abdabs, throwing their toys out the pram, or better still, bool 'em all down to the docks and sail 'em down the river and out to sea, and keelhaul the buggers and let the cat out of the bag and flog 'em under the command of the king with the cat-o'-nine-tails, and rub salt into their bloody wounds; that'll take the lead out of their pencils and wake the bastards up! In fact, hang 'em from the yardarm or make them walk the bloody plank, while we sit back scoffing Chalbert's fish and chips, laughing our tits off! Yeah, give 'em the bloody collywobbles and make 'em suffer! Make 'em sweat blood, shit and tears, and teach 'em a lesson they'll never forget!

Oh look, that's right, you're just like us old farts, aren't you? You piss-stained, soiled-armoured, snotty-nosed, blood-soaked, blubbering bunch of cowardly young twats!

Let's see how cool they are after that, with their stupid professional footballer haircuts and their bloody smart phones at £500 a pop, the same bloody price I paid for my first bleedin' house! Doesn't seem that bloody smart to me, fuckin' idiots! But no such luck and no bloody chance, as they sit on their constipated fart arses, slouching, pen-pushing, coffee-slurping, round-shouldered, pasty-faced, computer-button-pressing, pandiculating, prattling, pimpled pillocks, who've never done a hard day's work in their life, and wouldn't know one even if it bit 'em on the arse, like putting your back into it, grafting, bent sweating over a blistered hand-gripped shovel, digging a ditch or down a pit, toiling at the coalface, swinging a pick! Hard work never killed anyone, elbow grease, nose to the grindstone! Oh no, these lazy layabouts just want to stare at a bloody screen, knowing the price of everything and the value of nothing! Well, guess what? Stare at my boot as it gives you a bloody good kick up the arse!

Jesus!

Now, frame up, for fuck's sake, and pull your finger out!

John Cleese was right. They all need a damn good thrashing!

God, I really wish I had that cigar! I'd light it up, and this monochrome morgue as well, while I lay here mafted! Yeah, let's see who'd snatch the stick from me then, as they all ran around like headless chickens. Let 'em bloody try, as I puffed away, givin' 'em hell!

Smoking kills you, though, is what they'd say, like a poor old lorry driver friend of mine who died from cigarettes years ago, and he was only forty-eight, bless him. So sad! Yeah, he was unloading at the depot when a pallet of them fell on his head!

Oh, that reminds me, it's pizza for tea, with a bloody cup of water or orange cordial at best! Not a proper drink to wet your whistle, like a pint of hand-pulled Tetley's or a pint of mild; oh no, those days are gone, out on the town, pub crawling with my mates, drinking like a fish, getting smashed, wolf whistling, pinching arses and pullin' the birds, and suppin' up and fuckin' off, with change left over from a ten-bob note for a fish and chip supper!

Like that time when the lads were out on a balmy summer night's barmy bender, all of us completely kaylied, givin' it loads as we staggered home with a rendition of *Build Me Up Buttercup*, singing our hearts out as the dawn chorus joined in, and then a mate climbs up on stage, standing on a building site wall, and as he gets to, *'Just to let me down,'* the bloody thing collapses from under him, dropping him onto the foundations! Both legs and arms in casts for weeks, and me and the lads doubled up crying with laughter, and I haven't stopped since! As he said to me not long before he died, 'It was one of the best nights out ever, because I ended up getting absolutely plastered!'

'You hum it son, I'll play it.'

Halcyon days alright, and then bloody some! Best fucking ever!

Now all I do is give 'em the evil eye and tear them a new one with colourful words!

I'll tell you something else for nowt as well, I also used to drink and drive when I was a young whipper-snapper, all the bloody time; didn't give a shit about anyone or anything, including the rozzers, but not anymore, I jacked that malarkey in years ago because I was always spilling it!

'BADUM-TEESH!'

If you can dance to this, you can juggle with soot!

'BADUM-TEESH!'

Talking of drinking, I remember when all the lads and lasses were sat, cans in hand, watching England play in the 1970 football World Cup semi-final against Brazil, and at half-time, as we were all toasting Gordon Banks's stupendous save from Pele's header, an English teacher mate pointed out the importance of teaching kids spelling and English grammar:

'If you put beers in the fridge, you can enjoy a chilled out World Cup, but if you put bears in the fridge, you are arguably guaranteed a completely different experience!' he said, as he supped his lager and we all fell about.

'BADUM-TEESH!'

All things considered, though, I'm bloody well off when you come to think about it, as I watch these busy bloody bees buzzing around doing what exactly?

Swinging the bloody lead?

Shall I shout *'Fire!'* or cry for *'Help!'* or just lay here, a supine old man watching them scurry past my hospital bed?

I was young once, fitter than a fiddle, not laid out like a gasping cod, riddled with God knows what, fed up waiting to be fed!

She broke my heart, you know, dying on me like that! Never ever loved anyone or anything more, bigger than the world itself and everything in it, and now she lives buried deep within, my burning light a single candle that I hand-protect against the cold draft dark, as I walk up creaking stairs to her bed, holding her deflated frame closer still.

'Are you alright, love?' she whispers, her gentle words fluttering to me.

'I'm bloody great, love! No need to worry! Don't you want your tea?' I ask, swallowing hard and squeezing my cuddle around, cascading tears nuzzling her golden hair.

'Later, love. I'm just feeling a bit tired right now,' she says faintly, as I lay beside her atop the bedsheets.

'Alright then, you just rest a while.'

And she did.

Well, maybe it's time for me to go then, because none of them here are killing me with kindness. I'm just a pair of sunken eyes dulled with time, my body no longer the same, but not my brain, still sharp as a button as I lay here lame, metronome head turning, trying to catch their attention, a spectator at bloody

Wimbledon more like, looking left, right, left, right, left, right and left again.

'New balls please!'

Oh yes, and new everything else while you're at it! Or is that not part of the game?

'Hello Mr Grumpy Trousers, how's my favourite patient? Enjoying your day?' nurse asks, untucking my bedsheets as I nearly go into cardiac arrest from the shock!

Flaming Norah, where the hell did she come from? I wonder, as I load both barrels.

'Are you taking the bloody piss?' I snap.

'Yes, I'm about to!' nurse replies, smiling as she walks around my bed pulling the curtain and I sink back into the pillow with a sigh, surrendering to dextrous hands manipulating my waterworks.

Where Have All the Sparrows Gone?

Crouching in mud-caked trousers, like a grubby hide-and-seek champion mannequin, I reaffirm my grip on the damp string wrapped around my fingers, as I concentrate on the opposite end attached to the base of the vertical branch, holding up one end of an upturned cardboard box some ten feet away, in the middle of the back garden.

Have I put enough breadcrumbs out for these Old World sparrows? I wonder, as a Passer domesticus, one of three, hops across the sheening grass, moving closer towards what I hope is an irresistible sparrow-tempting snack.

Palms now clammy with sweat, I feel the painful onset of crouch-cramp contracting my muscles and numbing the pins and needles sensation prickling my legs, as pressure mounts for me to pull the string, felling the branch from its supporting position and instantly dropping the cardboard box, trapping a sparrow!

Wait, wait, ah, cramp! Bloody hell – oh, crap! I can't wait – the cramp! I need to pull it now, but not yet – ah, the pain! I can't wait – ah, flippin' heck! Yes, yes, it's nearly under the box! Oh, come on, move, move, just a bit more please, come on, MOVE! Yes, come on, move! Yes, yes, go for it, pull it now! YES! NOW!

I pull the string back fast with little resistance.

What? No!

I forgot about the slack, and instantly I pull back again harder, nearly wrenching my shoulder as the branch is finally yanked away with a fine string spray and the prefabricated trap falls, but the bird is quicker and has already taken flight with its two companions.

I stare at the stationary box, now laid upside down and empty in the middle of the lawn, like a poor man's podium as a flock of sparrows noisily congregate on our garage roof, overlooking the garden.

Oh, I know what you're all saying, because I actually speak Sparrow. Yeah, you're right, I missed again, but one day, one day soon, I will catch one of you... and do what? Kill it, pluck it, gut it, cook and eat it? Yuck! No, I don't want to hurt a sparrow, any sparrow. I just want to see if I can catch one; that's the game!

Until the next time, my brown-feathered little friends, and, unravelling the string from my hand, I drop it, flexing my fingers, and rise wincing like an old arthritic poacher, stretching limbs out, back arching, smiling as the free-flowing blood pleasurably restores the feeling to my legs and I cross the drizzled lawn to upturn the box and, picking up the stick, I start two-handed twisting it, slowly dragging the string towards me as I hand-wind it in, in a fashion. Then, holding the stick steady in my right hand, I use my left to spool it dripping around the wood wet and bundle it all inside the damp-based box and put the box in the shed, as sparrows swoop down from the 'dress circle' to squabble over the remnants of breadcrumbs, and forcibly heel-kicking my soiled, frayed, knotted black brogues off against the backdoor step, damp socks cold concrete stepping, I go back indoors to start my homework, and present my furrowed-browed mum with muddy school trousers.

Time Has Come

Not long now; not sure how long still breathing; still here, haven't gone!

Moment memories Rolodex-focussed, my time slipping away; people, places, faces, words unsaid, words pledged, words fled.

To go back, aged somewhere between eight and ten, paths worn already, my future somehow retrod more steady, or dragged down the same whirlpool eddy?

Start again? No thanks. It rains, get wet; not now, later, still wet. Follow my nose straight ahead, even turning, carried undulating along by the churning current, which way my life is yearning.

Seen things, felt stings, the joy my children bring; life's baton passed on, never ending love-sending.

Time to go? Taste of steak and eggs in my mouth, bread and butter, cup of tea, fish and chips, single malt whiskey, best to let it be; no sight-faded glaucoma regrets, as I drift off to birdsong, wind in the trees, cigar aroma, cauliflower cheese, smell of rain, glistening river trout, priest clout, storm clouds brewing, flowers' scent, breeze-flapping tent, sea water lapping, muddy river yacht crewing, sea fishing boat spewing, shimmering mackerel caught napping, sun-kissed sands, stomping flamenco feet and guitar plucking, clapping hands, caressing fingers, smiles abound, words whispered, eyes of brown, love blossoming, joyful mound, soft sound listening, invisible sparks, connect the dots, 'I love you' said a lot, unspoken words forgot, laughter, music and tears, yes, no, maybe not?

If it's dark, why all light? Time travelling in my head, wish it was me instead; I love you now and forever, space I filled dissipates to nought; still here, though, in what I made, not what I bought, but time spent, days and nights all past, compressed into one last breath, mirrored in water, reflecting me or you or them, my love, my children, my heart. Amen.

Of Land and Sea

I trek across vast, baked, shimmering plains, sparsely speckled trees in the mirage wet my only shade companions, all roofed in the blue.

Accompanied by swirling dust whipped up around, spinning guests of little sound but welcome friends my soul demands, as I walk in ferocious heat alone, a stranger in a strange land.

No science fiction landscape this, a world I know now closing down in the mist, vultures gathered looping higher up need me dead, winged black clouds always following as I led.

Fading light and dark mixed on palettes above all turn to brown when watered down, earth's epidermis.

Soil, clay and grass fashioned wet into walls over a man tall; sticks mud stuck a roof, flint-struck fire ventilated for air, protecting us from nature's relentless cold furnace!

Animal skin hide pulling mottled fur close at my neck, enveloped dark blankets a distant glimmering speck shackled to me, a point of reference dwindled down but there, I see.

Senses rise to the smell of salt in the air, light flickering now a dot, a future writing mark to end your plot and start afresh.

What?

Unknown, as gust-worn paths shown, sea now smashing on rocks crashing spent as I gather pace, light growing, muscles contract in my face; calling out, my family await as I secure my crimson-tipped spear in the ground and lay down my kill shouldered around, to greet the clan, fur-wrapped, warm, protected and soon to be fed, always my plan.

For we are you, just two hundred thousand years ago, fighting to survive is all we know, so futures unseen will blossom bright, not dull, as archaeologists brush dirt from around my disintegrated skull, shouting out their find, and I look up with wonder at my long lost relatives, human kind.

Bio

There Is Only Now is Glenn D. Webster's first anthology, comprising thirteen poems and five short stories.

Originally from Kingston Upon Hull, in East Yorkshire, Glenn has been inspired to capture 'real life' across its kaleidoscope of colours, focussing his artistic work on reflecting the world he sees and has experienced.

'If art dramatizes the reality of the world, then words define it.'

– Glenn D. Webster,
London,
November 2019

Credits

Isaac Newton (credited with the discovery of gravity in Grantham, UK 1666)

The International Space Station (The ISS is a space station in low Earth orbit, a joint project between space agencies: NASA, Roscosmos, JAXA, ESA, & CSA)

Pogo Stick (invented by Max Pohlig and Ernst Gottschall in Germany 1920)

The Tube (London underground public train network opened 1863)

Space Hopper (invented by Aquilino Cosani in Italy 1968)

Courvoisier (cognac brandy founded 1828 in Jarnac, France)

Montecristo No. 2 Cuban cigar (created in Cuba 1935)

Jaguar Cars (built in Coventry, UK from 1935)

Sainsbury's Supermarkets Ltd (UK supermarket chain - part of J Sainsbury plc)

Pickering Park (Kingston Upon Hull public park opened 1911)

Trumpton (British children's stop-motion TV series 1967)

Mars, HP & Irn-Bru (iconic brand names of a chocolate bar, a condiment food sauce and a Scottish carbonated soft drink respectively)

Crown Jewels of Queen Elizabeth II (housed in The Jewel House vault at the Tower of London 1207)

Superman (fictional comic book & film superhero published 1938)

Eurostar (London to Paris train service commenced 1994)

Sale of The Century hosted by *Nicholas Parsons* (British TV game show 1971-1983)

Grandad (Clive Dunn song by Herbie Flowers & Kenny Pickett 1970)

Sir Winston Churchill (British Prime Minister 1940-1945 & 1951-1955)

Bugs Bunny (animated cartoon character created 1930's)

Facebook (social networking service 2004)

John Kerry (American politician & 68th Secretary of State of the United States)

Jimmy Hill (English football professional & TV personality)

Brylcreem (British brand of men's hair styling products, started in Birmingham, UK 1928)

Henry Cavill (English actor)

Wendi Murdoch (ex-wife of media mogul Rupert Murdoch)

Joe 90 (British sci-fi TV series created by Gerry & Sylvia Anderson 1968-1969)

Glenfarclas Scottish single malt whisky (produced in Ballindalloch, Scotland since 1953)

Hoyo de Monterrey Double Corona Cuban cigar (produced in Cuba since 1865)

New York Mets beat the *Baltimore Orioles* (1969 Major League Baseball World Series in USA)

Bruce Forsyth (British stage & TV performer)

Noggin the Nog (British children's TV series character 1959–1965 & 1979–1980) and books by Oliver Postgate & Peter Firmin

Roscoe Conkling "Fatty" Arbuckle (American silent film actor 1887–1933)

The St. George's flag (designed with a red cross on a white field, adopted by England & the City of London 1190)

The Cybermen (fictional race of cyborgs & enemies of The Doctor in the British sci-fi TV programme Doctor Who 1966)

L.K.Bennett (international luxury fashion brand based in London UK)

Vivienne Westwood (iconic international British clothing brand)

The Matrix (1999 sci-fi action film starring Keanu Reeves)

Alien (1979 sci-fi horror film directed by Ridley Scott)

Peyton Place (1956 novel, 1957 film & 1960's U.S. TV soap opera)

Girl Guides (Girlguiding-The Guide Association. previously The Girl Guides Association started in UK by Robert Baden-Powel 1910)

Bye, Bye, Baby (Baby Goodbye) (Bay City Rollers, 1975. Bob Crewe & Bob Gaudio, 1965)

Rub-A-Dub-Dub (nursery rhyme first published end of 18th century)

Rockabye Baby (nursery rhyme 1765)

Granita (now defunct London Blair & Brown deal making restaurant 1994)

Blue Suede Shoes (Elvis, 1956. Carl Perkins, 1955)

Play School (BBC children's TV series 1964-1988)

Henry V (William Shakespeare 1623)

Oliver (1968 British musical drama film)

X Factor (British TV music competition franchise created by Simon Cowell & his company SYCO TV 2003)

Billy Smart's Circus (British touring circus 1946-1983)

Fawlty Towers (British TV comedy series starring John Cleese 1975-1979)

Sherwood Forest & Maid Marian (Ancient forest in Nottinghamshire, England, famous for its association with legendary English outlaw Robin Hood and his English folklore, 16th century love interest Maid Marian)

Laura Ashley (British textile design company founded 1953)

Nanny McPhee (2005 comedy fantasy film)

Bill and Ben the Flower Pot Men (BBC children's TV programme 1952-2002)

Geoffrey Capes (British shot putter, strongman & professional Highland Games competitor)

The Bitch Is Back (Elton John & Bernie Taupin, 1974)

Richard III (William Shakespeare, 1592)

Trevor McDonald (newsreader & journalist)

Taj Mahal (1653 Mausoleum in Agra, India)

Margaret Thatcher (British Prime Minister 1979-1990)

Brian May (Guitarist with British rock band Queen)

Sherlock Holmes (fictional private detective created by British author Sir Arthur Conan Doyle 1887)

Shakin' Stevens (British singer/songwriter)

The Terminator (1984 sci-fi action film starring Arnold Schwarzenegger)

Captain Scarlet and the Mysterons (British sci-fi TV series created by Gerry & Sylvia Anderson 1967 & 1968)

Campbell Meatballs (Campbell's US processed food & snack company 1869)

Queensbury Rules (The Marquess of Queensberry Rules code of boxing rules published London 1867)

Julius Caesar (William Shakespeare 1623)

'Never in the Field of Human Conflict' (a speech by Winston Churchill to the House of Commons in August 1940)

Henry V (William Shakespeare 1623)

'England expects that every man will do his duty' (from a message sent by Horatio Nelson aboard HMS Victory at the start of the Battle of Trafalgar 1805)

Rawhide (Frankie Laine song by Dimitri Tiomkin & Ned Washington 1958)

FA Cup (The Football Association Challenge Cup annual knockout football competition in men's domestic English football since 1871)

Silence Is Golden (The Tremeloes, 1967. Bob Gaudio & Bob Crewe, 1964)

Yorkshire Tea (Taylors of Harrogate since 1886)

McDonalds (McDonald's Corporation is an American fast food company, founded in 1940)

County Hospital (1932 film starring comedy duo Stan Laurel & Oliver Hardy)

Bedlam (London psychiatric hospital established in the fourteenth century)

Mission: Impossible (American action spy film series starring Tom Cruise as Ethan Hunt from 1996 to present based on original TV series)

I Spy With My Little Eye (nineteenth century English children's guessing game)

I Am What I Am (1983 Gloria Gaynor pop song by Jerry Herman)

GCSE (General Certificate of Secondary Education single-subject exam taken at aged 16 in England, Wales & Northern Ireland)

Who Wants To Be A Millionaire (international British TV game show franchise created by David Briggs, Mike Whitehill & Steven Knight)

Tsar Bomba thermonuclear weapon (1931 Soviet RDS-202 hydrogen bomb was the most powerful nuclear weapon ever created)

Dr Doolittle (children's book series by Hugh Lofting 1920 The Story of Doctor Doolittle & films, whose central character, Dr John Doolittle, can talk to animals)

'Belisha' beacon (1934 amber globe lamp containing a flashing light atop a pole, marking UK road pedestrian crossings, named after Leslie Hore-Belisha Minister of Transport 1934-1937)

Earl Grey (blended Chinese black tea originally presented to Charles Grey, 2nd Earl Grey 1803)

Carl Stewart (bespoke men's tailor of Wakefield, Yorkshire, UK for over fifty years)

Dan Nelson (shoemaker in Settle, Yorkshire, UK since 1752)

Dale End Cheddar (cheese made in Botton, Yorkshire, UK since 1977)

The Highway Code (UK Department for Transport, 1931, 2019 Edition)

Uber Eats (US online food ordering & delivery platform by Uber 2014)

Zebra Three (radio call sign of 1970s US TV cop series Starsky & Hutch)

NHS (National Health Service – UK publicly funded healthcare system 1948)

Z Cars (fictional British TV police drama series 1962-1978)

Pegasus, Pelican, Toucan, Puffin & Zebra (types of UK pedestrian road crossings where pedestrians are given priority)

Tickler cheese (made in Devon, UK since 2007)

Fortnum & Mason (upmarket department store in Piccadilly, London, established in 1707 by William Fortnum and Hugh Mason)

Mick Jagger (English lead singer of the Rolling Stones 1962-present)

Daisy Bell ('bicycle built for two' song by Harry Dacre 1892)

The Grand Old Duke of York (nursery rhyme 1642)

Peter O'Sullevan (BBC horse racing commentator)

Formica (plastic heat-resistant laminate invented in US in 1912)

Dr Who & the Tardis (British BBC sci-fi TV series with time travelling Dr & his time machine spacecraft 1963 to present)

Fly Me to The Moon (Frank Sinatra, 1964. Bart Howard, 1954)

NASA (National Aeronautics & Space Administration independent agency of the United States Federal Government responsible for civilian space program, aeronautics & aerospace research est. 1958)

The News of The World (weekly national tabloid newspaper published every Sunday in UK 1843-2011)

Battenberg (English marzipan covered jam sponge cake, with two-by-two check pattern alternately coloured pink and yellow 1884)

Amos Brearly (Woolpack landlord in Yorkshire based TV soap Emmerdale played by actor Ronald Magill 1972-1995)

Thunderbirds (British sci-fi TV series created by Gerry & Sylvia Anderson 1965-1966)

Thora Hird (English actress & comedienne of stage & screen)

Slim Pickens (American rodeo performer & film actor)

Dr Strangelove (Stanley Kubrick satirical Cold War film 1964)

Pinocchio (1883 novel & 1940 Walt Disney film)

Humpty Dumpty (English nursery rhyme 1797)

Pith helmet (lightweight cloth-covered helmet 1870)

Toys R Us (defunct international toy retailer founded 1948)

M1 (motorway connecting London to Leeds, UK 1959)

"Good-bye-ee!" (music hall song by R. P. Weston & Bert Lee 1917)

Baa, Baa, Black Sheep (English nursery rhyme dating from 1731)

Formula One (highest class of single-seater auto racing owned by the Formula One Group 1950)

Mersey Tunnels (connect the city of Liverpool with Wirral, under the River Mersey 1886).

Farley's Rusks (dry biscuit for babies manufactured by Farley's since 1880's)

Knees Up Mother Brown (song by Bert Lee & Harris Weston 1938)

'Birch rod' & 'cat o' nine tails' (British Royal Navy corporal punishment flogging implements used at sea in the 17th & 18th centuries)

'Keelhauling' & *'hanging from the yardarm'* (British Royal Navy forms of corporal punishment & execution used at sea in the 17th & 18th centuries)

'Walking the plank' (method of execution used at sea by forcing a person to walk off a plank of wood extended over the side of a ship in the 18th century)

Tetley's (English brewery company founded in 1822)

Build Me Up Buttercup (The Foundations, Mike d'Abo & Tony Macauley, 1968)

'You hum it son, I'll play it.' (Mr Shifter PG Tips British television commercial 1971)

World Cup (The FIFA World Cup is an international association football competition contested by the senior men's national teams every four years since 1930)

Gordon Banks (English professional footballer/ goalkeeper)

Pele (Brazilian professional footballer)

Wimbledon (Wimbledon Tennis Championships is the oldest tennis tournament in the world, held annually at the All England Club in Wimbledon, London, since 1877)

Rolodex (rotating file device for storing business contact information 1956)

If you would like to leave a review,

please visit the official Facebook page:

There Is Only Now by Glenn D. Webster